JoB

I zipped up the back of her dress.

She turned and backed away from me, moving closer to the wall.

"Which way do I look better?" she asked. "With or without? Take your time."

I went along with the game. I studied her face, and then I let my eyes drop. She was standing close to the wall, and I was more interested in what was happening at the base of that wall than in her ankles.

A red puddle was seeping from beneath the wallboards in a slowly widening circle.

VANISHING LADIES

ED McBAIN

Originally published under the pseudonym Richard Marsten

AVON BOOKS ◆ NEW YORK

This is for Jim Bohan—
who reads them all

This work was originally published under the pseudonym Richard Marsten

AVON BOOKS
A division of
The Hearst Corporation
105 Madison Avenue
New York, New York 10016

Copyright © 1957 by Richard Marsten
Published by arrangement with HUI Corporation
Library of Congress Catalog Card Number: 90-93387
ISBN: 0-380-71121-4

First Avon Books Printing: January 1991

AVON TRADEMARK REG. U.S. PAT. OFF. AND IN OTHER COUNTRIES, MARCA
REGISTRADA, HECHO EN U.S.A.

Printed in the U.S.A.

RA   10 9 8 7 6 5 4 3 2 1

Q: Do you swear to tell the truth, the whole truth, and nothing but the truth, so help you God?

A: I do.

Q: What is your name?

A: Philip Colby.

Q: How old are you, Mr. Colby?

A: Twenty-four.

Q: Do you live in this state?

A: No, sir. I live in the adjoining state.

Q: What first brought you to this state?

A: I came on vacation, sir.

Q: And when was that?

A: My vacation started on Monday morning, June 3rd.

Q: What sort of work do you do?

A: I'm a detective.

Q: A private detective?

A: No, sir. I work for the city. Right across the river, sir. The 23rd Precinct.

Q: But you were not at Sullivan's Point on police work, is that right?

A: That's right. I went to Sullivan's Point on vacation.

Q: What made you choose it as your vacation spot?

A: I didn't choose it, sir. Ann did.

Q: Ann?

A: Ann Grafton. My fiancée.

Q: I see. And when you chose Sullivan's Point, had you any idea at the time that you would become involved in police work?

A: That was the farthest thing from my mind, sir. I was looking forward to a vacation. The 23rd can . . . can become trying at times.

Q: But you nonetheless *did* become involved in police work?

A: Yes, sir, I did. That is . . . well, of a nonofficial nature.

Q: And were there any other policemen involved in this work?

A: Yes, sir. Detective Tony Mitchell. He works at the 23rd, too.

Q: Would you please tell the court exactly what happened?

A: Where do you want me to start, sir? It's a pretty involved thing, and—

Q: Start with the morning of June 3rd. Start with the day your vacation started.

A: Well . . .

1

I PICKED ANN UP AT NINE O'CLOCK.

Wait a minute, it must have been closer to nine-thirty. She lives with her father. Her mother is dead, you see. Her father was still home when I got there. He's usually off to work by about eight-thirty, but I think he was worried about Ann going off alone on a vacation with me. Not that he doesn't trust me or anything, but you know how it is when a girl has no mother, I guess a man worries about her.

We had a cup of coffee together while Ann finished dressing. I think she held off dressing on purpose, so that I'd have a chance to talk to her father before we left. I've got no reason to belive that except that she's usually pretty punctual, and she knew we were supposed to leave at nine. I guess Mr. Grafton got convinced over our coffee that I wasn't going to sell Ann into white slavery or anything. Anyway, we began talking about the chances the baseball teams had, and in a little while Ann came out of her room.

She's a pretty tall girl, I mean not a giant, but wearing heels she'd give most fellows a little trouble. She was wearing a white sun dress with bare shoulders and she looked pretty, but I'm prejudiced, I'm going to marry her someday.

Incidentally, I have to tell you what she looks like and what she was wearing because it's pretty important to what happened later on. She's got very black hair, you see, hair that's really black—as if it'd been dipped in India ink. And she's got wide brown eyes, and a good figure even though she's tall. You meet a lot of tall girls who look like telephone poles. Ann's not that way. Anyway, she was wear-

3

ing a white cotton dress, and she carried a straw bag and she wore these straw pumps with lucite heels.

She went over and kissed her father, and he put his arm around her shoulder and then turned to me and said, "Take care of her, Phil."

"I will," I promised. We shook hands then, and all three of us went down to the car together, Mr. Grafton carrying one of Ann's bags, and me carrying the other. The car we used for the vacation wasn't my own. I've got a '47 Plymouth. But one of the fellows on the squad, a detective named Burry O'Hare, drives a '53 Chevvy convertible, and he suggested I use that for the trip. As it turned out, the borrowed car wasn't such a good idea, but Burry of course didn't know what was going to happen and he was only trying to be nice.

We got under way at about ten that morning, the top down, and a nice breeze rushing through the city. We couldn't have chosen a more beautiful day to start our vacation if we'd tried. It was one of those days when even the city is comfortable even though the sun is shining to beat the band.

When we pulled away from the curb, Ann said, "Did you reassure Dad?"

"I told him I'm going to rape you as soon as we're over the bridge," I said.

"I'll bet you did."

"I did."

"And what did he say?"

"He said it couldn't happen to a nicer fellow."

"I agree with him."

"How do you like the car?"

"I love it," she said. "It was very nice of O'Hare."

"Sam Thompson offered me his car, too."

"Why didn't you take it?"

"Who wants a beat-up old '57 Cadillac?"

"Does he really drive a Caddy?"

"On a cop's salary?"

"All cops take graft. I happen to know."

"How come you're so smart?"

"I'm in love with a cop."

"That's the one thing I'm not going to like about this vacation."

"My being in love with a cop?"

"No. All the graft I'll miss while I'm gone."

I better explain here that we were kidding. I better explain, too, that Ann and I do a lot of kidding with each other, and I don't know if you want to hear all the kidding or not but the only way I can tell you what happened is to tell it to you as it happened. Anyway, it's that way in my mind, and it's mixed up enough as it is without trying to cut corners.

We drove crosstown to the bridge. The traffic was pretty light at that time of the morning, and we were in no real hurry, half the fun is getting there, you know. So we took our time crossing the bridge, watching a big liner coming in, billowing smoke all over the place. I guess we didn't really feel as if we were on our way until we hit your state after we crossed the bridge. With the river behind us, with the road stretching out ahead of us, with the sun beating down, and the wind streaming around the car, we really felt as if we were on our way. Ann reached over to turn on the radio, and then she squeezed my hand on the wheel and said, "Oh, Phil, I'm so happy."

"Before you get too happy," I told her, "get the map out of the glove compartment and let's see where we're going."

She fished out the map, and began reading off road numbers to me. I have to confess that I'm unfamiliar with your state. I was here once for a wedding, but I was only thirteen then and my father did the driving. I almost came again when some fellows wanted to see a burlesque, but somehow I caught a cold and couldn't make it.

Ann knew the state like a native, though. She'd spent a lot of time in the mountains as a kid and had traveled the roads a lot with her father. Which is where she got the idea for Sullivan's Point in the first place, I suppose.

"We should be there sometime this afternoon," she said. "Phil, you'll love it. It's the most beautiful spot in the world. These big pines, and this finger of land that juts out into the lake. I hope you swim."

"Does Buster Crabbe swim?" I asked.

"Yes, but does Phil Colby?"

"What kind of town is there?" I asked. "Or is there?"

"Sullivan's Corners," she said. "A few miles from the Point. Small. Quaint."

"Any big cities nearby?"

"Davistown," she said.

"Never heard of it."

"It's big."

She told me all about Davistown, and all about Sullivan's Corners and Sullivan's Point and her travelogue took us right to lunch time. We pulled into a Howard Johnson's, had a leisurely snack, and then hit the highway again. We drove steadily, and we talked, and we laughed, and it was beginning to feel like a vacation, if you know what I mean. Eventually we began picking up the Davistown signs, and then the Sullivan's Corners signs; twenty miles to Sullivan's Corners, ten miles, five miles, and then we passed a big sign saying "You are entering SULLIVAN'S CORNERS," and about a half mile past that, we picked up the state trooper. It was Ann who first spotted him.

"Darling," she crooned, "I don't want to upset you, but the minions of the law are on our trail."

I looked into the rearview mirror, just catching a glimpse of the blue uniform and the motorcycle. The trooper was riding some hundred yards behind us, away over on my right rear fender where he hoped my mirror wouldn't pick him up. I glanced at the speedometer.

"I'm only doing forty," I said to Ann.

The trooper pulled up and got off his bike. He was a tall, muscular fellow with a ruddy brown complexion. He wore sunglasses and when he got off the bike, he stretched and yawned and then casually strolled over to where I was sitting behind the wheel.

"Hi," he said.

"Hello."

"In a hurry?"

"No," I said.

"No? Maximum speed in this state is fifty miles per hour. You were tearing along at close to sixty-five."

For a moment, I couldn't believe I'd heard him correctly. I looked at his smiling face and I tried to read the eyes behind the tinted glasses.

"You're kidding," I said at last.

"Am I?" and he reached for the pinch pad.

"I'm a cop," I told him. "Besides, I was only doing forty."

"You were doing sixty-five, and I don't care if you're a judge," he said. "Let me have your license and registration."

"Look, officer. . . ."

"Let me have your license and registration!" he repeated, more sharply this time.

I dug into my wallet, making sure he saw the detective shield pinned to the inside leather, and then I handed him my license together with my acetate-encased police identification card and a card telling him I belonged to the Police Benevolent Association.

"Never mind the rest of the garbage," he told me. "I just want the license and registration."

"The rest of the garbage is part of the license," I said. "Maybe you'd better look at it."

He glanced at it. "So you're a Detective/3rd Grade," he said. "So what? In this state, we don't allow nobody to speed. Not even detectives from across the river." He handed my cards back, unfolded my license and then said, "Where's the registration?"

Up until that point, I still had some hope of getting out of this with a small lecture about law-enforcement officers speeding—which I hadn't been doing in the first place. When he mentioned the registration to me, though, it suddenly occurred to me that O'Hare and I had never even discussed it. Expecting the worst, I thumbed open the glove compartment.

"I borrowed this car," I said. "I hope the owner keeps his registration in the glove compartment."

"You borrowed it, huh?" the trooper said.

"Yes. From another detective."

"The registration in there?"

I was wading through the pile of junk O'Hare kept in

the glove compartment. There was a flashlight, a map of New Hampshire, a booklet advising him to "See the U.S.A. in His Chevrolet," several charge carbons from his gas station and—of all things—a .32.

"What's that?" the trooper said.

"Huh?" I said, knowing very well he wasn't referring to the map of New Hampshire.

"You got a license for that pistol?"

"I'm a peace officer," I said. "You know damn well I don't need a license to—"

"Whose gun is that?"

"Probably O'Hare's. He's the man I borrowed the car from."

"Did you find the registration?"

"No," I said dully.

"You'd better come along with me," the trooper said.

"Why?"

"How do I know this isn't a stolen car? How do I know those credentials you showed me aren't phony?"

"I showed you my tin," I said. "I sure as hell didn't buy that badge in the five and ten."

"You might have stolen that, too," the trooper said. "Follow me."

"Listen. . . ."

"I hate to hurl clichés," the trooper said, smiling, "but you can tell it to the judge." Then he stalked back to his bike as if he were ready to enter an International Motorcycle Competition.

"Damn idiot," I said.

"You *were* doing forty," Ann said. "I'm your witness."

"Sure, but whose word is the judge going to take? Mine or a cop's?"

"But darling," Ann said, "you *are* a cop."

"And why the hell didn't O'Hare leave the registration with me? Of all the stupid . . ."

"Our friend is taking off," Ann said.

2

THE JUSTICE OF THE PEACE WAS A MAN NAMED HANDY. He was a tall man in his early fifties with a magnificent mane of snow-white hair. He had pale blue eyes and a Cupid's bow mouth, and he held court in a log cabin about two hundred yards off the main highway. He undoubtedly lived in the cabin, and when we arrived he acted as if he'd invited us to his home for a cup of afternoon tea.

"Come in, come in," he said, and then to the trooper, "Afternoon, Fred."

Fred pulled off his gloves and his sunglasses and then followed us into the cabin. There was an old fireplace at one end of the room, around which George Washington and his troops had undoubtedly heated rum toddies. The j.p.'s credentials hung over the fireplace together with a Civil War saber that immediately put the Washington fantasy to rout. There was a long sofa and several easy chairs and an upright piano and a Grant Wood painting. A cut-glass cigarette box and ash tray rested on a coffee table before the sofa.

"Justice Handy," Fred said, "got an interesting one this time."

"Sit down," Handy said. "You and your wife make yourselves at home."

"We're not married," Ann said, and all at once all the precinct jokes about the Mann Act came into very vivid focus.

"Oh?" Fred said. Without the sunglasses covering them, his eyes were a frigid gray.

"What's the charge?" Handy asked, and somehow his

voice had grown sterner now that he knew Ann and I were not married.

"Speeding," Fred said. "Driving a vehicle without a registration. Impersonating a police officer. Violation of the Mann—"

"Now just hold it a minute," I said heatedly. "Let's just hold it a goddamn minute!"

"Is something wrong, son?" Handy said.

"Just about *everything* is," I said. "You'd better inform your motorcycle champ about the consequences of false arrest."

Handy chuckled a little. "No need to get sore at Fred," he said. "He only does his job." Handy scratched his head. "Speeding, huh?"

"I was doing forty miles an hour," I said.

"In a posted twenty-five-mile-per-hour zone," Fred put in.

"The highway speed limit is—"

"Not going through Sullivan's Corners. There's a sign just as you enter the town. Twenty-five miles per."

"By your own admission," Handy said, "you were speeding. "That's ten dollars. What about the rest of this?"

"I borrowed the car from a friend of mine. He's a detective, too. Call him at the 23rd Precinct and he'll clear this up right away."

"You a detective?" Handy asked, his brows raising.

"He claims to be one," Fred said. "There's a .32 in the glove compartment of that car outside."

"There's also a .38 in my hip pocket," I said. "Look, call Detective-Lieutenant Frank DeMorra at my squad." I dug into my wallet and came up with a card. "Here's the number. Tell him you picked up Phil Colby, one of his detectives, on a speeding charge. Ask him if I'm impersonating an officer, and ask him if I didn't borrow the car from Detective Burry O'Hare!"

"The Mann Act—" Fred started.

"The Mann Act doesn't mean beans unless you can

prove immorality," I said. "Why don't you put your sunglasses back on? They hide your dirty mind."

"Listen . . ." Fred started, and Handy turned to him with an outstretched palm.

"I reckon we ought to make that phone call, Fred," he said. He took the card from me, went to a dial phone near the fireplace, and then exchanged a few pleasantries with the operator before he got down to business. While he waited for someone at the 23rd to answer, he looked at me and said, "I've reversed the charges."

I nodded and said nothing.

In a few moments Handy said, "Hello. Let me talk to Lieutenant DeMorra, please." He paused, listening. "He's not in? When do you expect him?" Handy listened again, then said, "This is Justice Handy of Sullivan's Corners. We have a man here who claims he's a cop working out of your precinct. Name's Phil Colby. What's that? Oh, sure, sure." He covered the mouthpiece and turned to me. "He's connecting me with the Detective Division."

I let out a deep breath and waited. Ann sighed patiently.

"Hello?" Handy said. "This is Justice Oliver Handy, Sullivan's Corners. To whom am I speaking? Oh, how do you do, Detective Thompson?"

"That's Sam Thompson," I said. "Let me talk to him."

"Just a second," Handy said to me. "Detective Thompson, we've got a young man here named Phil Colby, say's he's a detective. What? He is? Well, that's good. He's driving a car he claims he borrowed," Handy said. "What? He did borrow it! From you? No? Well, then can I talk to whoever he did borrow it from?" Handy listened. I waited. "Not there, huh? Well, where is he? Out on a *what?* A plant? What's a . . ."

"A plant is—"

"When do you expect him back?" Handy asked. "Oh, I see. Well, that doesn't help this young fellow much."

"Look, will you let me talk to him?" I asked.

"Just a second," Handy said, and then he went back to the phone again. "I can't let him go until I talk to the fellow who owns that car,'' he said to Thompson. ''You understand that, don't you? Besides, he was speeding.''

''May I please talk to him?'' I asked.

''Just a second,'' Handy said to Thompson, ''he wants to talk to you.'' I practically ran across the room, and Handy gave me the phone.

''Hello, Sam,'' I said.

''Hello, Phil,'' Sam said. ''What's new?''

''Don't clown around, will you? I'm stuck here in a hick . . .'' I cut myself off, aware of the sudden stiffening of Handy's back.

''You shouldn't go tear-assing all over the countryside,'' Sam said. ''Tch-tch, boy, you should know better.''

''I was doing a big forty miles an hour!'' I said.

''In a stolen car, huh?''

''In O'Hare's car! Where the hell is O'Hare?''

''On a plant.''

''What plant? For Pete's sake . . .''

''Phil, I know it's an inconvenience to you, but we do try to run this little squad in your absence, you know. O'Hare is out trying to catch a burglar.''

''Well, when will he be back?''

''If I could consult the burglar, I'd give you a more definite answer. Unfortunately . . .''

''All right, all right. Will you have him call here as soon as he gets in?''

''What's the number?'' Sam asked.

''Sullivan's Corners 8-7520,'' I read from the dial plate.

''Hey, kid,'' Sam said.

''Yeah?''

''Have they got you on the Mann Act?'' he whispered.

''Go to hell,'' I said, and I hung up.

''Well?'' Handy asked.

''The man who owns the car will call as soon as he can. Do you want the ten dollars now or later?''

''Now's as good a time as any,'' Handy said, smiling happily.

* * *

The call from O'Hare did not come until one o'clock that morning. Ann was curled up on the sofa, half asleep. Handy was puffing on a pipe and telling me how good the fishing was at the Point. Fred had departed for the cinder tracks hours ago. When the phone rang, I leaped out of my chair. Handy motioned me to sit, and then he waddled across to it and lifted it from the receiver.

"Hello?" he said. "Yes, this is Justice Handy. Oh, how do you do, Detective O'Hare?" He listened, nodding. "Yes, that's right, that's right. Well, I'm certainly glad to hear that. Certainly, we'll release him at once. Thank you for . . . what's that? Oh, certainly, just a second." He covered the mouthpiece. "Wants to talk to you," he said.

I went to the phone. "Hello?"

"What's the idea stealing my car, feller?" O'Hare asked.

"Haven't you got anything to do but joke long distance at the city's expense?" I said, but I was smiling.

"You all squared away now?" O'Hare said.

"Yes. Thanks, Burry."

"Stupid of me not to think of the registration. Do you want me to mail it to you or something?"

"No, forget it. Lightning doesn't strike twice, you know. Did you get your burglar?"

"What? Oh, no, the son of a bitch laid off tonight. Maybe he's on vacation, too."

"Maybe. Burry, thanks again."

"Don't mention it, kid. Have a good time." He paused. "Just one thing . . ."

"Yeah?"

"The Mann Act," and then he hung up.

I was grinning from ear to ear when I went to the couch to wake Ann. She sat up as if I'd slapped her, and then said, "What! What is it?"

"We're free men," I said.

"And women," she added, wide awake. "Let's get out of here."

We shook hands with the genial Justice Handy and went out to the car. It was getting a little chilly, so I put up the

top and then pulled out the justice's wide gravel driveway.

"Thank God that's over," I said.

"Mmmm," Ann answered.

"Are you sleepy?"

"Yes."

"Why don't you rest? I'll wake you when we get to
Sullivan's Point."

"No," she said. "I'd rather stay awake now and sleep
during the night. Besides, I want to talk to you."

"What about?"

"You have a vile temper. I discovered that today."

"I know. The smallest things seem to upset me."

"You should learn to control yourself."

"I should, you're right."

"I love you, Phil," she said, quite serious all of a sudden.

"And I love you," I said.

"Do you miss the squad?"

"Miss it? Jesus, I feel as if I never left. All I've been
doing today is talking to the boys."

"We'll be there soon," Ann said. "It shouldn't take
more than a half-hour."

"Think we'll get a place to stay?"

"Oh, certainly," she said. "There are dozens of
places."

3

THE TOWN OF SULLIVAN'S CORNERS WAS CLOSED TIGHT when we pulled into it. I hadn't exactly expected the blare of neon, not after Ann's earlier description of the town's size, but I had hoped to see a living soul or two.

The town lay at the base of a steep hill. The hill came as a surprise because it was immediately around a sharp bend in the highway. You made the turn, and suddenly the road was dropping away in front of you, and your headlights picked out nothing but the blackness of the night and then a sign stating "SULLIVAN'S CORNERS, Speed Limit 25 mph," now they tell me. It was difficult to keep the Chevvy down to twenty-five, especially on a roller-coaster hill like that one, but I remembered my recently concluded brush with the local law and burned Burry's brake lining for all it was worth. I suppose I was being a little overcautious. Fred and his cohorts, like everything else in Sullivan's Corners, were undoubtedly dead asleep.

The town seemed to start as soon as the hill ended. There was a short plateau at the bottom of the hill, and a traffic circle sat in the center of the plateau, ringed with a closed bar, a closed luncheonette, a closed hotel with a "No Vacancy" sign, and a closed billiards parlor. There were no road signs at the circle. The only indication of any traffic instruction was a blinking yellow caution light strung across the street high above the empty police booth in the center of the circle. I stopped the car and leaned out of the window.

The town was dead still. There were crickets and katy-dids and an occasional animal sound from somewhere off in the distance, but that was all. The caution light

15

blinked its gaudy yellow into the Chevvy. The air was cold and heavy with moisture. I could see my breath pluming from my mouth. "Where to?" I asked Ann.

"The way I remember it," she said, "you drive through town and then take a turn down to the Point."

"Where are these dozens of places you mentioned?"

"They should be on the road to the Point."

I put the Chevvy in gear, swung around the circle and drove through town, sticking to the twenty-five-mile-per-hour speed. The town had a temporary look to it. The main street was lined with the shops you find in any town, the grocers, and the butchers, and the dry goods stores, but they all gave the feeling of having been thrown up in haste, a feeling that they could have been disassembled in five seconds flat and taken underground in an atom bomb attack. There was, too, if a town can give out such a feeling at one o'clock in the morning, a sense of unfriendliness. The 23rd Precinct territory was certainly no happy valley. It was crammed full of humanity living under the worst conditions invented by humans for humans. It was dirty, and it was corrupt, and it overflowed with pimps, pushers, prostitutes, hoods, ex-cons, and petty thieves—but it was part of the greatest city in the world, and it beat like the heart-pump of that city and there was rich warm blood there and laughter in spite of the filth. There were muggings and knifings in the 23rd, yes. But there were also lovers walking hand in hand or stealing a kiss on a rooftop skylight. There were police locks on almost every apartment door in the 23rd, yes. But there were *people* behind those doors. There were shadows in the 23rd, and it wasn't the safest place in the world to walk at night. But the sun shone during the day, and if the faces that turned up to the sun were dirty, they were nonetheless laughing.

I had the feeling that Sullivan's Corners did not laugh very much. I had the feeling that the shadows clinging to the narrow alleyways between the clapboard front buildings did not disappear with the sun. That's silly, I know. Any small town might look menacing in the early hours of the morning. Any small town might look unfriendly.

Then, too, I have the advantage of being able to second-guess the thing in the light of what happened later at Sullivan's Point and in the town of Sullivan's Corners. But what I felt that night had nothing to do with what was going to happen in the next few hours. I remember the feeling distinctly, and I remember turning up the car window because I felt suddenly chilled.

We almost missed the small sign nailed to one of the telephone poles. I was, in fact, past the cutoff when Ann said, "There it is, Phil."

"Where?"

"We just passed it."

I threw the car into reverse and backed up. The sign was no wider than six inches and no longer than the space it required to sloppily print Sullivan's Point. One end of the sign had been shaped into a point so that it formed an arrow. The road it pointed to was as black as Hitler's heart.

"Very inviting-looking," I said.

"There are lights as we go on," Ann promised. "And places to stay."

I looked at the speedometer and then tooled the Chevvy onto the cutoff. The road was narrow and winding and hadn't seen a paving contractor since it was laid by the Mohicans. We bumped and jostled along, raising dust every inch of the way. I looked at the speedometer again. We'd come four miles, and there still was not a light.

"There *used* to be places," Ann said in a small voice. "Maybe they haven't opened for the season yet. This is only June, you know."

"Yes, I know."

"Are you angry with me, Phil?"

"No," I said honestly. "No, Ann. It's just . . . well, you've had a rough day, and you only had a sandwich for lunch and . . . well, I was hoping we'd find a nice place. You must be exhausted."

"I am tired," she said. "What do you want to do?"

"Well, let's follow the road to the end. I couldn't turn back here anyway. It's too damn narrow."

"I'm sorry," she said.

"Don't be silly. If there's nothing here, we can always go on to Davistown. You said that was pretty big."

"Yes, it is."

"Fine. We're sure to get something there."

"All right, Phil." I could feel sleep crowding the edge of her voice. She sighed heavily, a sigh of utter exhaustion. Unconsciously, I pressed my foot more firmly against the accelerator.

We passed several motels during the next six miles, but they were all closed, no lights, no people, no cars. I was anxious to reach the end of the road and the Point now, because—even though I could have made my turn at any one of the motel courts—I was determined to see "these big pines, and this finger of land that juts out into the lake." It was a foolish, kid way to start thinking, and I'd have saved Ann and myself a lot of unasked-for trouble if I'd just made my turn and headed for Davistown. But I wanted the satisfaction of at least having reached the place we'd started out for in spite of all the garbage we'd put up with that day. It didn't make much difference to Ann because she was rapidly becoming unconscious on the seat beside me. She'd rested her head on my shoulder and pulled her legs up under her. I knew she was almost out because her skirt had pulled back over her knees during the tucking-of-legs operation and she hadn't bothered to shove it back down again. She's got good legs, Ann, but I wasn't too interested in them at the moment because the road was still bumpy and winding and narrow and dusty and because I was filled with this compulsion to reach the Point, take a sniff of the pines and the lake, and then get back to civilization.

The light startled me, and I guess if I hadn't seen the light I'd have driven straight into the lake and drowned us both. When I saw the light, I automatically reached for the brake pedal and that was when my headlights picked out the dock and the water. I stopped the car about ten feet from the dock, and then turned on the seat.

"Ann?"

Ann didn't answer. Ann was dead asleep, her skirt pulled

back over her knees, her head angled onto my shoulder. I eased out of the car, resting her head on the back of the seat, closing the door gently so I wouldn't wake her. The light was coming from a cabin at the end of a wide pea-gravel court. A football goal-post sign straddled the court entrance. The sign carried the one word: MOTEL.

I was looking up at the sign when the door to the cabin opened, spilling a patch of amber onto the gravel. A man was standing in the doorway. A shotgun was in his hands.

"Who is it?" he shouted.

"Put up the gun," I said. "I'm looking for a place to stay."

"Who are you?" He still hadn't moved from the doorway. He was a short, squat guy silhouetted by the light so that I couldn't see his face. He seemed to be bald, and he seemed to be in his undershirt, with his suspenders unhitched and hanging down over his trousers.

"My name's Phil Colby," I said.

"I don't know you, Colby," he answered.

"I don't know you either. I'll want two cabins. Are you open?"

"Why two cabins?"

"There's a girl with me," I said. "My fiancée."

There was a long pause while the man in the gray flannel undershirt digested what I'd just said. He put the shotgun down inside the doorway then and said, "You wait there," and then went into the cabin. When he came out a moment later, his suspenders were back on his shoulders and he carried a long six-cell flashlight. He sprayed a circle of light onto the gravel, walking with his head down, his face still in shadows.

"My name's Barter," he said when he reached me. "Mike Barter."

I extended my hand but either he didn't see it in the darkness or he simply didn't feel like taking it.

"Nice meeting you, Mr. Barter."

"Where's the girl?" Barter asked.

"In the car."

He walked toward the car, keeping the circle of light on

the ground ahead of him. When he got to the car, he lifted
the flash and stuck it in the window.

"Hey!" I said. "She's sleeping. Get that flash out of the
car."

He didn't seem to hear me. He leaned halfway into the
car and by the time I got to him the light had swung down
and was on Ann's exposed legs. The skirt had hiked up a
little higher, so that her thigh showed in the harsh glare
of the flash. I clamped my hand onto Barter's shoulder and
swung him around.

"Are you convinced?" I said tightly.

"Convinced about what?"

"That she's a girl?"

"Pretty," he said.

"Thanks."

"I think I've got two cabins for you."

I could see his face now. It was a round face covered
with beard stubble. It had a broad flat nose and small
glowing black eyes embedded deep in layers of flesh. I
didn't like the face.

"Adjoining cabins," I said.

"Sure," he answered.

"With bath," I said.

"Shower's in back of the office," Barter said. "We're
building some cabins with showers in 'em but they won't
be ready 'til July 4th. That's when my season starts. Of-
ficially, we ain't even open yet."

"We won't be staying that long," I told him.

"How long did you plan on?"

I looked at his face again, and I still didn't like it. "Just
overnight," I said.

"Mmmm. Well, shower's still in back of the office. You
interested?"

I was debating at that point whether or not to climb back
into the car and forget all about Mr. Barter's motel or settle
for what would certainly not be a Waldorf suite. It seemed
important to me, however, to get Ann into a bed. That is,
get her asleep in a bed. Her *own* bed, I mean. I mean . . .

"We'll stay," I told Barter.

"Seven dollars for each cabin," he said. "In advance."

"Fine."

"Want to come up to the office?" I glanced at the car and Barter caught it. "Don't worry about the girl. She's all right where she is."

"Sure," I said. I followed Barter up to the cabin with the light. There was the inevitable sign announcing the fact that this was the MOTEL OFFICE. The inside of the cabin was done in knotty-pine wallboard. There was a desk, and a closet, and a few filing cabinets, and a chair. On the wall behind the desk was a nude picture of Marilyn Monroe under which hung the excuse for the picture: a minuscule calendar. Some eager male had scribbled what he'd like to do with Marilyn in pencil across her belly. Barter opened a drawer in the desk, pulled out a register and turned it so that it faced me.

"Just sign in for yourself. Girl can sign in when you leave in the morning." He saw the puzzled look on my face. "It's for the record. Anybody renting a cabin's supposed to sign the register. Unless you want to check in as Mr. and Mrs., in which case I'll give you one cabin and you can sign for both of you."

"We'll take two cabins," I said.

"To each his own," Barter said. "Then she'll have to sign the register in the morning."

"All right," I said. I signed and then fished out my wallet. Barter went to the closet to get some towels. When he came back to me, my fourteen dollars was on the desk, and my wallet was back in my pocket.

"I'm giving you twelve and thirteen," he said.

"Are they adjoining?"

"Well, not exactly. Eleven and twelve are adjoining. Thirteen's got a little driveway between it and twelve."

"Then give me eleven and twelve."

"Can't. Somebody's in eleven."

"Then give me thirteen and fourteen."

"Somebody's in fourteen, too."

"All right," I said, disgusted. "All right."

"If you want to start getting your stuff, I'll take the towels up."

"Fine," I said.

We went out of the office and he trudged up the path with his flashlight and then a cabin light splashed on, and I saw the number "13" under the light and then Barter entered the cabin with his towels. I went to the car and leaned in, "Ann," I whispered.

"Mmmm?"

"Ann, are you awake?"

"Urhmmm," she said.

"Ann, I've got a place for us to stay the night."

"Good," she said.

"Do you want to get out of the car now?"

Ann didn't answer.

"Honey?"

Still no answer. I sighed, went around to her side of the car, opened the door, and then reached in for her. She hardly stirred when I picked her up. I braced myself, hiked her a little higher in my arms as soon as I was clear of the car, and then went up toward the cabins. Barter was just coming out of number 13.

"Got it all tidied up," he said. "Sheets was changed this afternoon, and I just now put clean towels in." He looked at Ann, studying her hard. "Dead asleep, ain't she?"

"We've had a long trip," I said.

"Pretty girl," he answered, his eyes never leaving her face. Then, "Why don't you put her in 13? I'll get 12 ready for you meanwhile."

"Fine," I said. I climbed the steps and went into the cabin. It sported the same knotty-pine wallboard as the office. There were two windows and a bed and a maple dresser and a sink and a closet. I went to the bed, dropped Ann down on it, and then yanked the covers from under her. I noticed there was a kerosene burner in the cabin, but there seemed to be plenty of blankets on the bed, and I doubted if Ann would need the burner. I took off her shoes, left the cabin light on, and then went back to the car for her bags. She was still asleep when I returned to the cabin. I put both bags in the closets, and then I went to the bed. I propped her into a sitting position, unzipped her dress down the back and somehow managed to get her out of it, in spite of the fact that a sleeping girl is all dangling arms and legs. I left her in her half-slip and brassiere, pulling the blankets to her throat. I hung the white dress on a hanger in the closet. Her purse, which I'd taken from the car, I left on the dresser. I flicked out the light then and walked outside.

Barter was standing just outside the cabin door, a leer on his face. The leer made me wonder just how long he'd been standing there.

"All tucked in?" he asked, one eyebrow raised.

"All tucked in," I said curtly, and I closed Ann's door.

"Your cabin's ready now," he said. I walked across the narrow gravel driveway which separated 12 and 13. Barter had left the light on, and I could see the clean towels he'd put on the rack near the sink.

"Are those showers working?" I asked.

"Running water all the time," Barter said proudly.

"Good. I'll take one and then turn in."

"Suit yourself," he said. He paused, then added, "Wear a robe to and from the shower, will you? I have other guests."

"Well," I said, "I usually run around stark naked."

"Huh?" Barter asked.

"Singing Christmas carols," I added.

"Well," Barter said, completely unfazed by my high-handed attempt at wit, *"here* you got to wear a robe."

"It won't be easy," I said, and I left him worrying that one while I went t the car. I took my valise from the back seat, and I took O'Hare's .32 from the glove compartment. Then I looked up and went back to number 12. Barter was gone. A light burning in the office told me where he was. I went into the cabin, closed the door, undressed, and then took a robe from the valise. I picked up a bar of soap from the sink, a towel from the rack, and then I put on a pair of loafers and started for the shower. The office light was out now, and there was hardly any moon. I found my way along the gravel path as best I could.

The shower was a simple wooden coffin set on end. I opened the door, took off the robe and hung it outside with the towel, and then backed off while I experimented with the water. The cold water was frigid. The hot water was cold. I left the cold water off entirely, turned on the hot, and planned to make this a really quick wash. I was under the shower for about two minutes when I heard a truck starting in the woods somewhere behind the motel.

The sound was unmistakably that of a truck, and I remember wondering what a truck was doing in the woods at that hour of the morning, but I didn't give it too much thought. The truck hit the gravel and did a little maneuvering, and then it stopped and I heard a few doors slamming, and a few whispered voices, and then the truck headlights splashed across the door of the shower, illuminating the booth for just a moment. The driver threw the truck into second, navigating the small rise leading to the road, and then the wheel noises told me the truck had left the motel gravel for the dirt road. I kept listening. In a few minutes, the engine sound was just a hum, and then it faded completely.

I rinsed off all the soap, opened the door a crack and pulled in the towel. There was a nip in the air, and the shower booth collected every draft in the neighborhood and left me shivering. I dried myself quickly and then pulled in the robe and got into it. I put on my loafers, then picked up the bar of soap and headed back for number 12. There wasn't a light burning anywhere in the motel. On impulse, I stopped at cabin number 13, half-hoping Ann had awakened and would feel like talking a little. From outside the door, I whispered, "Ann?"

There was no answer. I opened the door a crack and poked my head into the darkness. I couldn't even see the bed, no less Ann.

"Ann?" I whispered again.

Again, there was no answer. Gently, I closed the door and walked across the driveway to my own cabin. I opened the door, reached inside for the light switch, and turned it on.

I was closing the door behind me when I saw the girl on the bed.

4

YOU GET USED TO HOOKERS IN THE 23RD PRECINCT.

You get used to them because they're a part of the scenery. They roam all over the precinct. They sit in bars, and they stand on street corners or in hallways, and after a while you get to know everyone who's hustling. "Hello, Ida," you'll say, or "Hello, Fritzie," or like that. You watch them to make sure they don't hustle in the bars because you can revoke a man's license for that. You watch them, too, to make sure their old man isn't a mugger who's just looking for a sailor from downtown, a john with a few sheets to the wind. Prostitution in our city isn't government-protected the way it is in Panama. But the vice cops don't always overexert themselves and a lot of policemen feel that sex is a thing best let alone.

The hookers in the 23rd Precinct don't look at all like movie versions of "loose women." They don't wear skin-tight satin dresses, and they don't plaster make-up all over their faces, and they don't swing red purses, and they very rarely walk with suggestive wiggles. They're usually pretty conservatively and stylishly dressed. They wear lipstick and once in a while some face powder. Generally, the younger ones look like clean-cut high school girls except when they're dressed up to visit a friend downtown, on which occasions they accumulate years with the high-heeled pumps they don. Sex with the hookers in the 23rd is a business. You may find their talk a little rough because they speak of their business in terms which have become connected with it over the years—but only among them-

25

selves. With their gentlemen friends, their sex talk is usually refined and probably educational.

I only mention the hookers in my precinct to point up a comparison.

The girl on my bed, you see, in cabin number 12 at Sullivan's Point was obviously a hooker.

She was a redhead.

Her face was ghastly white with the covering layers of make-up it carried.

Her lips were a garish red, the lipstick extended above and beyond the lip line to exaggerate the size of her mouth.

Her dress was extremely low cut so that her small breasts in their tight brassiere were bunched together and uplifted like crowded passengers in an ascending balloon.

The dress was purple. It was not lavender, not violet, but purple. The brightest, gaudiest, shiniest purple I'd ever seen in my life.

Her legs were crossed, and the dress was pulled to a few shades above her knees.

She wore no stockings.

She wore black patent high-heeled pumps with ankle straps.

She jiggled one foot, and there was a gold ankle bracelet on that foot.

If she was more than seventeen years old, I'd have been willing to eat all of Mike Barter's gravel driveway.

We looked at each other for a few minutes, and then she said, "Hi." She drew out the word, gave it a throaty sound, tried to pack into that single word all the allure of Cleopatra floating down the Nile on a barge.

"You've got the wrong cabin, haven't you?" I said.

"Have I?" she asked. She was still the *femme fatale*, throwing her curves with all the subtlety of a Little League pitcher.

"I think so," I answered. As far as I was concerned, I didn't know what or who this little girl was, and I didn't particularly care. I was sleepy. I wanted to go to bed. Alone.

"I *don't* think so," she answered.

"Well, I'd enjoy kicking the problem around with you," I said, "but I'm really too tired to argue."

"*Would* you enjoy kicking it around with me?" she asked, a knowing smile on her mouth.

"I think the best way to solve this," I said, "is to run up to the office a minute. If you wandered into the wrong cabin . . ."

"You look young," the girl said, "but you can't be *that* young." She studied me for a moment. "I like blonds," she added. "Blond-haired men send me."

She was still blithely unaware of the fact that I wasn't interested, nor did she fully realize just how *far* I intended to send her.

"Little girl," I said, "I don't think you un—"

"Blanche," she corrected, raising one eyebrow.

"All right, Blanche. Why don't you go home, Blanche?"

"I want to stay here."

"So do I."

"That can be arranged."

"No, Blanche, it can't."

"Why not?"

"I snore. I'd keep you awake."

"That's the whole idea," she said.

"Honey . . ."

"See," she said, leaping on the word, "you're getting affectionate already."

"I'll get so affectionate in the next ten minutes that I'm liable to kick you out of here on your ass."

Blanche giggled. "That sounds like fun."

"Look," I said, "you've drawn a blank. Chalk it up to experience and go home."

"I'm staying," she said flatly.

"I'd hate like hell to really scare you," I said.

"Go ahead. Really scare me."

"I'm a cop."

She studied me levelly for a moment and then said, "Sure. And I'm a robber. Let's play cops and robbers."

"Do I have to show the tin?"

"The what?"

I sighed heavily. "Blanche, let's play this straight. I don't know who steered you to this cabin, but whoever did made a mistake. I didn't order anything. I'm not interested. I'm tired, I'm sleepy, I don't like redheads, and I don't like seventeen-year-old kids who should be home reading comic books. Now don't force me to get tough, and don't force me—"

"I wouldn't dream of forcing you," she said coyly.

"Oh, for Christ's sake!" I exploded.

"Now you're swearing."

"How old are you, Blanche?"

"Why?"

"I'm interested."

"I figured you'd eventually get interested. I'm over eighteen. Stop worrying."

"When were you born?"

"What?"

"When were you born?"

Blanche chewed her lip while she did a little addition. "January of nineteen thirty-nine," she said at last.

"Give or take a few years."

"You're a real worry wart. Have I asked you how old you are?"

"Where do you live, Blanche?"

"In town."

"Sullivan's Corners?"

"The Corners? I wouldn't be caught dead in a Maidenform bra there."

"Where then?"

"Davistown." She paused. "It's a real big city."

"I'm sure it is."

"It *is*," she said, suddenly sparking with adolescent rebellion. "How would you know? You ever been there?"

"No," I admitted.

"Then okay."

"Okay."

"If we're going to sit and talk, let's make ourselves comfortable," she said, her anger suddenly dissipating.

"We're not going to sit and talk," I told her. "I'm going to sleep. You're going home to that huge metropolis of yours."

"I couldn't get there tonight if I wanted to. I haven't got a car." She reached behind her for the zipper on her dress.

"Hold it right there, Blanche," I said. I fished into my pocket and pulled out my wallet. I let it fall open to where my shield was pinned to the leather. Blanche studied it with mild interest.

"A detective, huh?" she asked casually.

"I said I was a cop."

"So what? Are you on duty?"

"Twenty-four hours a day."

"Don't give me that bull," she said. She looked at the shield again. "You ain't even from this state. You got no authority here."

"I imagine I can pull a little weight with the local police," I said, remembering my earlier brush with the trooper and the j.p. and doubting my statement even as I said it.

"You think so?" Blanche said, raising the eyebrow again, her voice edged with sarcasm.

"I think so," I bluffed.

"What would you charge me with?"

"Soliciting."

"Anybody in this room expose her privates?"

"Not yet," I said.

"Then climb off your soapbox." She paused and then grinned. "Your scare didn't scare me. You're a cop, okay. Ain't cops human?"

"We're human."

"Good. Let's start acting that way."

We both fell silent. I didn't know what she was thinking, but I was trying to figure a new approach. I suppose I could have picked her up and thrown her out but she was, after all, a kid—and I'm not in the habit of knocking kids around.

"Let's take it from the top," I said.

"Let's."

"One: what do you want here?"

"I thought that was obvious."

"Two: how much?" The reason I asked this was simple. If I could establish her price, I was willing to give her the money to get rid of her.

Blanche grinned. "First time, the treat's on me," she said.

"Oh?"

"It begins to sound interestinger and interestinger, doesn't it?" she asked.

"It begins to sound fishier and fishier," I told her. "Why me?"

"Why not? I told you. I like blond men."

"Blond *cops?*"

"Blond *men*. Cops are men, same as any others."

"And your business is men, huh?"

"My business is men."

"You're a little young to be in business for yourself, aren't you?"

"American initiative," she said. "Supply and demand. There's a big demand."

"Then why give it away?"

"Mister, you should never learn never to look a gift horse, you know what I mean?"

"Sister," I said, "you should learn about leading horses to water."

"Huh?"

"Forget it."

"Good. I'm glad that's settled." She unzipped her dress and started shrugging out of it.

"The minute that hits the floor, I dial the local cops," I said.

The dress hit the floor, and she stepped out of it, grinning. "Ain't no phone," she told me.

She was surprisingly well-built. The tight dress had somehow made her look thinner than she actually was. She owned good hips and firm thighs, and since she hadn't removed her high-heeled shoes her legs were long and shapely and tapering. She wore white cotton pants and a white cotton bra. Her flesh, below the neck, had a healthy glow to it. Her face, covered with make-up, looked sickly against it.

"Nice?" she asked, still grinning.

"Lovely," I said. "Put on your dress and get the hell out."

"I'm staying," she said. "Let's get that straight. I'm not leaving. I'm sleeping in this cabin tonight." She tossed her red tresses in the direction of the bed. "In that bed."

"My fiancée is in the cabin next door," I said.

"She scares me, too," Blanche said.

"She's a big girl. She's liable to be a little tougher with you than I care to be."

"I can handle big girls and big boys too," Blanche said. She looked at me archly and said, "Admit it. I'm a nice package, ain't I?"

"Sure," I said.

"And I came gift-wrapped. God, but some men are lucky."

"Go wash your face," I said.

"I always do," she answered, and she wiggled over to the sink. I sat on the edge of the bed and watched her, somewhat bewildered. I honestly didn't know what to do next. I was toying with the idea of taking a blanket and going to sleep in the woods outside. I was also fighting to keep my eyes open. The water splashed into the sink with monotonous regularity. Finally, Blanche began drying herself. When she pulled the towel away from her face, she looked more like fifteen than the eighteen she claimed. I began to feel like a father about to hear a recounting of his daughter's evening at the junior high school prom.

"Clean?" she asked.

"Very clean."

"I hate that junk on my face."

"Then why do you wear it?"

"I don't know," she said. She seemed to be thinking this over for a moment. "What's your name, anyway?"

"Phil," I said.

"You don't look like a Phil. There's a Phil in Davistown but he's a jerk. You look more like a . . . a Richard."

"That's a good name," I said.

"Sure it is. Phil's okay, too. Don't take offense."

"I didn't."

She put her hands on her hips. "Well, here we are, Phil. Alone at last."

"Blanche," I said, "you're going to be very much alone in the next few minutes. I'm taking a blanket and going outside."

"You'll get eaten up alive. We've got mosquitoes here that break the sound barrier."

"I'll chance it."

"You'd be safer in here."

"I prefer the mosquitoes."

"We can work this out, you know. I'm really not that horrible."

"You're very nice," I said.

"But?"

"But I'm sleepy."

"I'll let you sleep. Get undressed, go ahead. I won't bother you."

"Why don't you be a good kid and get out of here? Come on, huh? Let's cut the nonsense."

"I can't, Phil," she said seriously.

"Why not?"

She looked at me hard and long, the guileless penetrating stare of a very young girl. And then she shook her head slightly and the grin came back, the hard grin of a professional prostitute. "Do you sleep in pajamas?" she asked, the eye-brow cocked. "I'll bet you're cute."

"You're not leaving?"

"Sorry," she said, impishly.

"I suppose I could go wake up Barter and tell him there's a big grinning woodchuck in my cabin."

"If I know Mike, he'll come join us," Blanche said, grinning.

"The boys back at the 23rd will never believe this," I said, shaking my head. I sighed, got off the bed and then took one of the blankets from where it was folded near the foot. Blanche sidled over to the door and leaned against it. I turned with the blanket in my hands.

"Let's don't play games," I said.

"Let's do," she answered.

I took a few steps toward her. "Kid, I'm being very nice," I said. "If you weren't so young, and if I weren't so kind, I'd kick you out just the way you are and give the mosquitoes a feast. I'm being nice, you understand? *I'm* leaving instead. I paid for this cabin, but I'm leaving. So don't start playing games because I'm mighty damn tired and I'm liable to snap."

"You look good when you get sore," Blanche said.

"Get away from the door," I said tiredly.

"Make me," she said, grinning.

I didn't grin back. "Get away from the door," I said.

Blanche tossed her head and grinned. I reached out for her, dropping the blanket. She ducked inside my extended hand then threw herself against me and wrapped her arms around my waist, locking her fingers behind me in the small of my back.

"It's not so bad when you get close to it," she said. She lifted her face. "Why don't you kiss me? My face is clean."

"Your mind isn't," I said. I reached behind me and broke the lock of her hands. She tried to reach the door again, but I sideswiped her with my arm, and she reeled back into the cabin. I picked up the blanket and headed for the door again.

"You're strong," she said softly.

"Good night," I said.

"Wait. Phil, please. Wait." Her voiced sounded very small. I turned to face her.

"What is it?"

"Don't . . . don't go yet. Please."

"We've been through this already."

"I'm sorry. I shouldn't have . . . this isn't right, what I'm doing."

"Damn right it isn't."

"I guess . . . I guess I'm not so good at it. I should have . . . have made you want to stay."

"Don't underestimate yourself," I said.

"Look, Phil . . . I . . . please, I have to talk to someone. Please stay a minute."

"Go ahead. Talk."

"Just like that?"

"How else?"

"Do you . . . do you have anything to drink?"

"No."

"Oh. I . . . I thought I could use a drink."

"You probably can."

"Do you hate me?"

"Not particularly."

"A little?"

"Not even a little. My father taught me to look for good in people. It gets difficult sometimes, but I still try."

Blanche laughed a short, hard laugh. "Do you see anything good in me?"

"I see a girl of sixteen or seventeen who's in 'way over her head."

"I'm really eighteen, Phil." Blanche paused. "Well, not really. I'll be eighteen next month."

"You're still in over your head. Why don't you be smart about this, Blanche? Why don't you go back to Davistown and get married and have kids and raise petunias?"

"I don't know if that's what I want."

"Who sent you here tonight?"

"I just came. Of my own accord."

"How'd you know I was in this cabin?"

"I saw you when you went to the shower. So I came over."

"Why?"

"I wanted to."

"Why?"

"I don't know."

"Where were you when you saw me going to the shower?"

"Cabin number 3. That's in the back."

"What were you doing there?"

"I took the cabin for the night."

"Why?"

"I wanted a place to sleep."

"What made you change your mind?"

"About sleeping?" Blanche shrugged. "I saw you, I guess."

"And?"

"And you looked nice. I figured I'd spend the night with you?"

"Free?"

"Yes."

"How long have you been hooking?"

"About a year now."

"Why'd you start?"

"I don't know."

"You must be doing pretty well if you can afford to be so generous with your time."

"I told you. I liked you. I saw you and I liked you."

"I could hardly see my hand in front of my face out there. But you *saw* me and liked me, huh?"

"I saw you when you stepped outside. In the light."

"That's an amazing feat, considering the fact that I turned out the light before I left the cabin."

Blanche was silent.

"Now what's the real story?" I asked.

"I . . . I was frightened," she said.

"Of what?"

"Just the darkness, I guess. I saw you . . ."

"We're back to that again, huh?"

"I saw you when you first pulled up, damnit!"

"Then you know there's a girl with me?"

Blanche hesitated. "Yes," she said at last. "I know there's a girl with you."

"But that didn't matter, huh?"

"I figured she was your sister. Hell, she took a separate cabin."

"She's not my sister. We're going to be married."

"Anyway, I was frightened," Blanche said. "When I

saw you . . . you looked strong. So I came over. I thought
. . . I thought you'd be glad to see me." She paused.
"Weren't you even a little glad to see me?"

"No," I said flatly.

There was the sound of a high-powered automobile outside. The headlights splashed across the cabin window.
Blanche went to the window quickly. She watched for a
moment. The car cut its engine, and Blanche let the cur-
tain fall.

"I've got an idea," I said.

"What?"

"Go back to cabin number 3. Sleep well. In the morning if you're still here, Ann and I will drive you to Davistown. How does that sound?"

"I think my idea is better. Don't I tempt you even a
little?"

"You try too hard," I said.

"Yeah," she answered noncommittally. She chewed her
lower lip, thinking. "Can't we talk a little more? I hate to
go back."

"If we talk a little more, it'll be morning," I said.
"Come on, be a good kid."

"I suppose you're right. Besides . . ." She was ready
to say more, but she cut herself off.

"You'll leave?" I said.

"Sure. I'm sorry if I caused you any trouble."

"No, not at all," I said, hoping the relief wasn't shining
out all over my face. "Put on your dress, okay? Come on,
get dressed."

Her dress was still lying on the floor, a limp puddle of
purple passion. She scooped it up, dusted it off gingerly,
and then said, "You sure? I'm a nice package."

"I'm sure you're delicious," I said. "But not tonight."

"Josephine," she added, and then she giggled and
pulled the dress over her head. She smoothed it down over
her hips and her thighs, and then turned so that she was
facing the wall which divided my cabin from cabin number 11 next door. With her back to me, she said, "Zip it
up, will you?"

I zipped up the back of her dress.

She turned and backed away from me, moving closer to the wall.

"Which way do I look better?" she asked. "With or without? Take your time. Examine it carefully."

I went along with the game. I studied her face, and then I let my eyes drop. When they reached her ankles, my eyes stopped. She was standing close to the wall, and I was more interested in what was happening at the base of that wall than in her ankles.

Because close to the exact spot where the wall met the wooden floor, a red puddle was seeping from beneath the wallboards in a slowly widening circle.

5

"WHAT'S THE MA . . . ?" BLANCHE STARTED, AND THEN
she saw what I was looking at. Her face went white, almost as white as it had looked when it was plastered with
make-up. Her hand went to her mouth, and I thought I'd
hear a full-bodied scream, but no sound came from her
throat. She moved away from the wall quickly, as if the
spreading red smear were a Martian fungus which would
envelop and destroy her.

I walked to the wall quickly. I stooped down and
touched the red smear with my fingers. It was sticky and
cold. It seeped steadily from a crack in the wall, seeped
steadily from cabin number 11.

I got to my feet.

"Where are you going?" Blanche asked. There was
panic in her eyes now, a sick panic that made her lips
tremble.

"Next door," I said. I started for the door, and then I
went back to the dresser where I'd unceremoniously
dumped my trousers before heading for the shower. I took
my .38 and holster from the back pocket. I unholstered
the gun, threw off the safety, and then walked out of the
cabin.

There were no lights in 11. I climbed the steps and
rapped on the door with the butt of the .38.

"Open up!" I said.

I tried the door. Usually a door will give just slightly
when you twist the knob and lean on it. This door didn't
budge an inch. It was sealed more tightly than an Egyptian
crypt. I rapped on the door again. "Open up, goddam-

nit!'' I yelled. I heard footsteps behind me on the gravel, and I swung around, bringing up the .38. It was Blanche.

"What are you doing?" she said. "Are you crazy?"

"Crazy enough to know blood when I see it," I said. I pounded on the door again, and then I stopped pounding and came down off the steps. I went into the cabin next door to 11, the cabin that was mine for the night, the cabin with a 12 under the light, the cabin with a spreading puddle of blood on the floor. Blanche followed me in.

"That's not blood," she said. "You're crazy."

"Am I?" I put the .38 down on the dresser. "I'm going to take off this robe and put on my pants," I said. "You'd better leave."

"I'll stay," she answered.

"Your choice," I told her. I took off the robe and flipped it onto the bed. I pulled on a pair of undershorts, a tee shirt, and my trousers. Then I opened the dresser drawer and took O'Hare's .32 from where I'd left it. I stuck that in my left hip pocket. I picked up the .38, and *that* stayed in my hand. Then I started for the door again.

"Where are you going now?" Blanche asked. She was very upset. Her mouth was still trembling, and she could hardly keep her hands still.

"Up to see Mike Barter. He should have a key for that cabin."

"Why don't you stop acting like a cop?" she shouted. "A little red paint—"

"Red paint, my foot!" I said, and I went out onto the gravel.

The light from 12 splashed onto the gravel for a good ten feet before darkness swallowed the path. I walked at a fast clip, and behind me I could hear Blanche struggling with her high heels on the loose stones. There was a hard-top Cadillac parked in front of the office. It hadn't been there before, so I assumed it was the car which had pulled in while I was talking to Blanche in my cabin. There was no light coming from the office. I banged on the door.

"Barter!" I yelled. "Mike Barter!"

There was no answer. I began to bang on the door again,

and it suddenly occurred to me that I hadn't even tried the
knob. I don't know if your mind ever has short-circuited
like that, where the simple obvious things don't seem to
register, where everything seems to be an insurmountable
problem that has to be solved the hard way. The easy way
was trying the door knob. I tried it, and the door swung
open.

The office was pitch black. I groped for a light switch.
The first thing I saw when the lights came on was Marilyn
Monroe's handwritten belly.

"Barter!" I yelled.

My voice echoed throughout the cabin and the woods.
There was an interior door in the office, and I opened that
and walked into a small surprise. The surprise shouldn't
really have been one because motel owners do have to live
some place. But I hadn't expected a full-fledged apartment
tacked to the back of the office. Nor had I expected one
quite as sumptuous as this. I had, to be truthful, expected
the door to open on a closet or something.

It opened on a big living room covered with a plush
rug, furnished in expensive modern. It opened on a hi-fi
cabinet about a hundred miles long with a bar at one end
of it, the bar stocked with stuff I couldn't afford to pro-
nounce. There were doors leading from the living room.
There was more.

I only tried one of the doors. I wasn't house-hunting at
the moment. The door I tried opened on a bedroom. There
was a large double bed, and a circular white rug thick
enough to swallow up a safari. There were dressers and
mirrors and a night table and a chaise longue, and a frilly
woman's dressing table. A woman's pink mules rested at
the foot of the dressing table. The sheets on the bed were
made of blue silk, and the white monogram on them read
SBR. The sheets were as out of place in this neck of the
woods as Satan would have been at the last supper. The
covers on the bed were turned down, but the bed had not
been slept in.

The room was something of a mess.

Dresser drawers were open, clothing askew. The closet

door was open, and there were a lot of empty hangers, and a lot of hangers on the floor, and also one dress which had probably slipped from a hanger.

I left the light burning on the night table, just the way I'd found it. I walked into the living room, and maybe I should have tried the other doors, but I didn't. When you're making a search, it should be a careful one. That's elementary police work. But I was searching for a key, so I left the closed doors closed, and I walked through the living room and into the office again.

I went directly to the desk, figuring Barter was most likely to keep his keys in it somewhere. I pulled open the top drawer.

Mike Barter kept a well-oiled .45, a few bills from a milk company, a letter from a linen supply outfit, a blotter, and a few broken pencils. He did not keep his keys in that top drawer. I spread a handkerchief on my open palm, picked up the .45, and sniffed the barrel. Whatever else Mike Barter had done, he had not recently fired the automatic. I put the gun back in the drawer, closed it, and was opening the second drawer when Blanche came into the cabin.

I swung around. "Where does Barter keep his keys?" I asked. "Do you know?"

"No. Listen to me," she said.

"Don't give me the red paint story again, or—"

Her eyes blazed at me. For a second, she didn't look seventeen any more. She looked as old as Methuselah, and her eyes held all the secrets of the universe. "Listen to me," she said, and there was a tight wire-thin edge to her voice. "Get out," she said. "Get out of here. Forget Barter and forget that blood. Just get out."

"I'm getting into that cabin," I said.

"You're a fool," she answered.

I began digging through the second drawer. There were paper clips and stationery and more pencils, but no keys. I slammed the drawer shut. Blanche glanced swiftly toward the interior office door.

"Phil," she said softly, "please . . . take my advice. Don't bother with this. Get out. Please."

"Ann and I are staying right here until . . ."

I stopped.

"Ann!" I said, and I could feel everything inside me go cold. For two heartbeats I stood welded behind the desk. Then I turned and ran out past Blanche, and onto the gravel driveway, and then to cabin number 13. I ran up the steps. I didn't knock. I simply threw open the door and flicked on the light.

The cabin was empty.

6

IT WAS THREE O'CLOCK IN THE MORNING.

I was at Sullivan's Point in a state which was not my home state, in a cabin where I'd left a girl a little while ago.

The cabin was empty.

Ann was not in the bed.

The bed looked as if it had never been slept in.

There was no baggage in the open closet.

There was no purse on the dresser.

The white dress I'd hung in the closet was gone.

Ann's shoes were not at the foot of the bed where I'd dropped them.

The cabin was empty and silent, and it screamed with its silence and its emptiness. I panicked. I stood there, and I panicked because I could only think of the over-coffee talk I'd had with Mr. Grafton the morning before, and the assurance I'd given him that I would take care of his daughter. I could only think of that and the bloodstain on the floor of my own cabin, and so I panicked and I don't know how many minutes rushed by before I got control of myself. I remember staring down at the .38 in my fist and then I remember running out of the cabin and shouting "Blanche!" and getting no answer.

And then the car lights hit me in the face.

The car was a very old one, and it rattled into the court, swinging in a wide curve toward the office, its headlights knocking long tunnels into the darkness. I shielded my eyes from the glare, and then the car ground to a stop some ten feet from me, and Mike Barter climbed out. Whoever was driving the car did not move from behind the wheel.

"What's the matter?" Barter asked, seeing the gun in my hand. "Something wrong?"

"Where were you?" I asked.

"Why, over to Hez's place. What's the matter?"

"Where's the key to eleven?"

"Why? Who wants to know?"

"I do."

There must have been more menace in my voice than I thought. Barter looked at me cautiously and then barely turned his head and said, "Hez? Hezekiah!"

There was movement on the front seat. I saw the fellow named Hezekiah slide from behind the wheel and then leap from the car. He was a big man, at least six-four and weighing all of two hundred and ten. He moved with an animal grace, though, first springing out of the car and then effortlessly striding over to where we stood.

"Trouble, Mr. Barter?" he asked, and his voice rumbled up from somewhere deep inside a chest like a wine cellar.

"No trouble, Hez," I said. "Stay right where you are. This gun has no friends."

Hez stopped and looked at the gun. He had blue eyes, and they darted to Barter and then back to the .38 in my hand. His eyes were set in an angular face—sloping cheeks and flat surface planes and square tight lips—which looked like an exercise in geometry.

"Get the key, Barter," I said.

"I'll get no such damn thing," he answered. "Happens there's a guest in eleven."

"It's the guest who interests me," I said.

"Why don't you mind your own business and go back to your cabin?"

"Because the guest may *be* my business. It so happens I'm missing the girl I came in with."

Barter looked at me, and then he looked at Hez, and then he looked at me again. Very quietly, he said, "What girl?"

"The girl I—"

I stopped short. It was my turn to look at all the faces. Hez's face was blank. Barter's face was a cold mask. "Cut the comedy," I said tightly.

"Your name's Colby, ain't it?" Barter said. "You're in twelve."

"You know damn well where I am, and you know the girl was in—"

"You checked in alone," Barter said flatly.

It was quiet for a few seconds. I could hear the sound of the crickets, and the sound of the water lapping against the shore of the lake. Very calmly, very quietly, I said, "What's the bit?"

"You checked in alone," Barter repeated. "What you trying to pull here, anyway?"

"Look, you son of a bitch," I said, "don't give me any of *that* crap! *I* know I checked in with a girl, and *you* know I did, and if you don't produce the key to eleven in about three seconds, I'm going to forget I'm a cop and start squeezing this trigger for all it's worth."

"A cop?" Barter asked. He glanced rapidly at Hez. "You're a cop?"

"Damn right, I am. One, Barter."

"How was I supposed to know you're a cop?"

"Two, Barter."

"I've got the key in my pocket," he said. "I'll take you up to eleven, but you won't find nothing there. You especially won't find no girl, because you didn't come with no girl. I don't know what the hell you're trying to pull."

"Make him show his badge, Mr. Barter," Hez said.

"Yeah, how 'bout that?" Barter said.

I took out my wallet and flipped it open to the shield.

"That ain't worth nothing in this state," Barter said.

"This gun is worth a lot in *any* state," I told him.

Barter looked at the .38. "Come on," he said. "I'll show you that cabin."

I let Barter and Hez walk ahead of me to the cabin. Barter took out a big ring of keys and inserted one into the lock. He threw open the door then, flicked on the light, and stood aside.

"Inside," I said. "You, too, Hez."

They went into eleven, and I went in behind them. I was afraid of what I might find, and relieved when I didn't find it. There was no body on the floor. There was nobody in the cabin. But nobody.

"Satisfied?" Barter asked.

"Not yet," I said. "Get over on the bed, both of you. Hurry up. Face down, hands up on the pillows."

"You're not gonna get away with this, feller," Barter said. "I don't know who or what you think you are, but we've got cops in this state, too, you know."

"On the bed," I said.

Barter climbed up onto the bed, and then Hez climbed up beside him. They made a nice couple. Together, they rolled over onto their stomachs and put their hands up onto the pillows.

"Don't get off the bed," I said. "I'll shoot whoever tries it first."

"Tough bastard," Barter muttered.

"Yeah," I said. "I'm a tough bastard."

I went over to the wall separating 11 from my cabin. I covered every inch of the baseboard and found no sign of blood at all. Then I came to the closet. The closet was toward the front of the cabin, and it suddenly occurred to me that the blood seeping through the wall had been near the front of my cabin, too.

I didn't want to open that closet door.

I opened it.

There was a lot of blood on the floor. The floor sloped toward the wall gently, so that it took the blood a long time to run toward the wall and then to seep through the crack in the wallboards into my cabin. A long time—so that whatever had made that blood puddle could have been taken away long before any blood had shown in the adjoining cabin.

"Come here, Barter," I said.

Barter scrambled off the bed and waddled over to where

I was standing just outside the open closet door. He looked in at the blood. He didn't say anything.

"How about it?"

"What is it?" he said.

"Blood."

"I don't know anything about it," he said. "I rented this cabin about six o'clock last night. Fellow from Vermont. What he done here, I don't know nothing about."

"What was the fellow's name?"

"Don't remember. It's in the book."

"Now tell me, what happened to the girl I brought here?"

"You didn't bring no girl here," Barter said.

"That's your story, huh?"

"That's the truth," Barter said emphatically.

I kept myself calm. I kept myself very calm, considering. "Barter," I said, "you're lying. I don't know why, but you're lying. There was a girl with me, and I have a witness who saw us check in together."

"Who's your witness?" Barter said.

"A girl named Blanche."

"Blanche?" Barter said. "I don't know nobody named Blanche."

"She rented cabin number three from you. She was in there all night. She saw us check in."

"You got girls on the brain, ain't you?" Barter said. "Ain't nobody in number three but a guy who checked in after supper."

"Somebody took the girl, and her luggage, and her clothes out of the cabin while—"

"Which girl you talking about now?"

"I'm talking about the girl I brought here, damnit!"

"I see," Barter said, smiling at Hez who had craned his neck around from the bed. "And what cabin was she supposed to have checked into!"

"Number thirteen."

"Why don't we just take a little stroll up to thirteen right now?" Barter said. " 'Course, that's if you're finished with your detective work in here."

"I'm finished," I said. "I want to give thirteen a closer look, anyway."

"All right if Hez gets up off the bed?" Barter asked, smiling. This was all very comical to him. This was all simply side-splitting to him.

"Come on, Hez," I said, and I waved the .38 at him.

We went out of the cabin and then over to 13. The motel was alive with light now, amber spilling from 11, 12 and 13, all in a row like nuns carrying votive candles. The door to 13 was closed. Barter climbed the steps and knocked.

"There's no one in there," I said. "Just open—" and just then the door opened.

A tall thin man stood in the doorframe.

His chest and his feet were bare. He was wearing the trousers to a brown worsted suit. He was as wiry as a Con Edison cable, and a patch of black hair clung to his breast bone, and two halos of the same hair ringed the nipples of his pectorals. His eyes were blue, and his hair was a mussed brown, and he looked at us in mild surprise and said, "Yes?"

"Sorry to trouble you, sir," Barter said. "Is everything all right?"

"Why, yes," the man said. He looked at my .38. "Say, what is this?" he asked.

"How long have you been in this cabin?" I asked.

"Who the hell are you?"

"My name's Phil Colby," I said. "How long have you been in this cabin?"

The man nodded, as if the name had meant something to him. "I checked in at about eight," he said. "Why?"

"You checked in shit!" I said. "Move aside!"

The man moved into the doorframe, blocking my path. "Just hold it a minute, sonny," he said. "My wife happens to be in bed."

"Your *what!*"

"My wife. What the hell's so strange about that? Listen, are you nuts or something?"

"Get out of my way," I said. "I want to see your wife!"

"Listen, what kind of a place is this?" the man said to Barter. "For Pete's sake, I never—"

I shoved him aside and moved into the cabin. Two green plaid suitcases rested on the floor near the dresser. There was a woman in the bed, and she sat erect when I barged into the room, pulling the sheet to her throat. She had long blond hair and green eyes, and the eyes opened wide, and I thought she would scream, but she only opened her mouth and stared at me. She wore no make-up, and her face looked as if she might have been sleeping, except for the fact that her eyes weren't tired.

"What's your name?" I asked.

"Who wants to know?" she answered.

I turned to her husband who had come into the cabin after me. "What's your name?"

"Joe," he said.

"Joe what?"

"Joe Carlisle. This is my wife."

"What's her name?"

Carlisle paused, and then he turned to the blonde. The blonde gave a slight smile.

"Stephanie," she said. "Stephanie Carlisle."

"How long have you been in this cabin, Stephanie?"

"Since about eight o'clock. Why?"

I nodded, turned away from the bed, and went to the closet. I opened the door and looked inside. The closet was full of clothes. A woman's coat, two dresses, a nightgown, some skirts, and some blouses.

"Where are *your* clothes, Joe?" I asked.

"I travel light," he said.

"Let's see your identification."

"What for?"

"Let me see it!"

"I haven't got any."

"You drove here, didn't you?"

"Yes, but . . ."

"Let me see your driver's license."

Carlisle shrugged. "I hadn't thought of that," he said. He went to the dresser and took his wallet from where it lay alongside a watch and a key case. He opened the wallet and handed me his license.

"You a cop?" he asked.

"Yes."

"This a purity drive or something? We're married, you know."

The name on the license was Joseph Carlisle. The address was in Davistown. I handed the license back to him, and then I went to the dresser. I opened the top drawer. It was full of Stephanie's lingerie. The other two drawers were empty.

"Those bags open, Joe?" I said.

"I guess so. Why do . . ."

I walked to the suitcases and unsnapped the first one. It was empty. The second one was empty too. I closed the bags and walked into the bathroom. A comb rested on the sink. I opened the medicine cabinet. It was empty. I left the bathroom and went into the big room again. Carlisle's shirt, tie, and jacket were thrown over the wooden chair. His shoes were on the floor under the chair, and his socks were balled inside the shoes. Stephanie's dress and underwear were heaped on the seat of the chair. She caught my eye.

"The nylon stuff is mine," she said, smiling.

"Thanks," I told her. "And where do you keep your purse?"

The smile dropped from her face. I could feel the gears clicking inside her head for just about two seconds, and then the smile came back and she said, "I must have left it in the car."

I turned to Carlisle. "And where's the car?"

"I parked it up near the office."

"The Caddy?"

"Yes."

"Then you didn't pull in more than a half-hour ago."

"You're mistaken," he said. "We checked in at eight."

"Do you plan on staying long?"

"Just . . . a few days."

"We came for the fishing," Stephanie put in.

"Is that why the two dresses in the closet are cocktail gowns?"

"Well . . ." she started, and I turned to Carlisle again.

"You going to fish in your brown worsted suit, Joe?"

"I told you," he said, "I travel light. I usually travel with only what I'm wearing."

"No dungarees? No old flannel shirt? You mean you're going to fish in a good suit? You're going to . . . ?"

His face turned hard. "I'll fish in whatever I like," he said.

"Except troubled waters."

Barter smiled. "Think we can let these people get back to sleep now?" he asked.

"Sure," I said. "And you can take me around to your other cabins, Barter."

"I run a business, you know," he said. "It don't help business to go around waking up people in the middle of the night."

"I don't imagine it does," I said dryly. "Come on."

Carlisle remembered to be indignant again as we were leaving. "You've got a lot of nerve barging in here like this," he said.

"Go to hell," I told him.

Barter and Hez were waiting for me at the foot of the steps. "Where do you want to start?" Barter asked.

"With number one. And then right down the line."

"Suit yourself. Most of the cabins is empty anyhow."

"Then why were you so worried about waking up guests?"

"Well, some of them's got guests," he mumbled, and then he led me in a semi-circle around number 13 and to the string of cabins thrown onto the hillside. The first two cabins were empty.

Number 3, the cabin Blanche said she'd occupied, was dark when we approached it.

Barter knocked.

"Who is it?" a man's voice answered.

"Me," Barter said. "Mike Barter."

"Oh. Just a second." A light went on, and someone

cursed, and then we waited a few minutes, and then footsteps approached the door. The door opened. The man
standing in the doorframe was in his undershorts. They
were gaily patterned shorts, a wolf's head making up the
main motif. The wolves all over the shorts were baying.
They were baying at shapely female legs which formed the
secondary theme of the pattern. The man wearing the
shorts may or may not have been a wolf. He looked more
like a den mother.

He was at least sixty, and his head was bald, and his
eyes were red-rimmed, and the paunch he carried hung
over some of the wolves which is probably why they were
baying.

The first thing he said was, "Where's . . ." and then
he saw me and shut up.

"Where's who?" I said.

The red-rimmed eyes flicked with intelligence. The old
man grinned. "Not *who,*" he said, "but *what!* I was asking Mr. Barter where the towels he promised me were."

"Shucks, clean slipped my mind," Barter said, snapping his fingers. "Mind if we come in, sir?"

"If you don't mind my greeting you in my underwear,"
he said.

He stepped aside, and we all trotted into the cabin. My
eyes went to the bed. There were two pillows on it, and
both had been slept on. I went into the bathroom and
looked at the towels. One of them had a lipstick smear.

"Let's check the other cabins," I said.

On the way out, Barter turned to the old man. "I'll get
you those clean towels," he promised.

Cabins 4, 5 and 6 were empty. A dark-haired girl
opened the door to number 7. She wore a blue bathrobe,
and she seemed surprised to see Barter. She also seemed
about to say something until she saw me. She kept her silence instead, looking to Barter questioningly.

"Sorry to disturb you and your husband, ma'am," Barter said. "I wonder if we might come in?"

The girl studied Barter, and then her eyes darted to me.
She didn't ask, "What for?" or "What the hell do you

mean?'' or anything else you'd expect from a surprised housewife at a motel being awakened in the middle of the night. She simply stepped aside and let us pass.

''Where's your husband?'' I asked.

She looked into the room as if she'd temporarily misplaced him.

''Must be in the john.'' She paused. ''Want me to get him?''

''Never mind,'' I said. ''Come on, Barter.''

We left the girl. She stared after us as we went down the path. Then she closed the door.

''Rest of the cabins is empty,'' Barter said. ''Want to see them?''

''You've been right about everything so far, haven't you?'' I said.

''Sure.''

''Then why bother looking at them?''

''Just the way I feel about it,'' Barter said. ''Why don't you go back to your own cabin and get a good night's sleep? You'll see, in the morning you'll wake up feeling better.''

''Um-huh,'' I said, and I started for my car. ''Except there's one thing I've got to do first.''

''What's that?'' Barter asked, smiling.

''I've got to go get the police,'' I told him.

7

THE CADILLAC CARLISLE HAD ARRIVED IN WAS STILL parked up near the office. I was half-tempted to open the door and look for Stephanie's purse, but I hardly thought it necessary. There are some things you sense instinctively in detective work, some things you automatically know. I'm a new detective, and my nose isn't as sensitive as the noses of guys like Burry O'Hare or Tony Mitchell who have been plying their trade for quite some time. Burry or Tony can simply look at a man and tell you whether or not he's honest. I can't do that yet. It comes from being around thieves, I guess, and it's only natural. Crime detection is a line of work, the same as any other line of work. When a jeweler's been handling gems long enough, he doesn't have to put in his eyepiece to differentiate the real from the phony. He can tell from the feel of the gem, and the sheen and the glitter. Thieves glitter, too.

Maybe Stephanie's purse *was* in that Cadillac.

Maybe I only imagined putting Ann in cabin number 13. Maybe I was nuts and everybody else was telling the truth. Maybe Carlisle did travel light, and maybe he and his wife checked into number 13 at eight o'clock. And maybe the sun rises in the west.

But a woman's purse is like a man's wallet. You take it with you. When you're getting out of a car, it's the first thing you reach for. It contains all the paraphernalia of a woman's trade. It's as essential to her as her left breast.

I put the convertible into reverse and backed up around the Caddy. My headlights picked up Barter walking toward the office. I don't know what he was thinking, but he was walking very fast with his head down, Hezekiah following behind him like an elongated shadow.

I headed directly for the log cabin of Justice Oliver Handy. I could have called the police by telephone, I suppose, but it was close to 4:00 A.M., and only God knew where I'd find a telephone booth.

I was wide awake, you understand. Wide awake and beyond the first agony of paralyzed panic. It seemed idiotic to me that I could have ever believed the blood in cabin number 11 belonged to Ann. Ann was gone and—I was sure—in danger, but I no longer believed she was dead. The danger, it seemed to me, was very real. If she was gone, there was a good reason for her absence, and the blood in cabin 11 seemed like a very logical and strong reason. People don't voluntarily bleed on a closet floor. Where there's blood, there's danger.

So I drove quickly and with purpose. I was a cop and I was being tolerated. But the shield I carried was weightless, and I needed the heavy hand of the local law to put the machinery of fear in motion.

Fear.

A very helpful thing to a cop. Everybody's got a skeleton some place, and nobody wants it dragged into the middle of the living room during tea. Fear urges the innocent man to protect his own skeleton by telling the truth about someone else's bag of bones. Fear can lead the guilty man to panic, and panic is the great undoer among criminals.

There was a little bit of fear on the face of Oliver Handy when he opened the door for me. The fear surprised me. Perhaps he was just the kind of man who automatically becomes frightened when someone raps on his door in the wee small hours. But there had been a light burning in the cabin when I pulled up, and when Handy opened the door—even though he was in pajamas and robe—he did not have the look of a man who had come directly from a warm bed. There was something else strange about the way he admitted me. I knocked, and he didn't ask "Who's there?" or anything. He came straight to the door, opened

it, and said, "Oh, Colby"—almost as if he'd been expecting me.

"I'm glad you remember me," I said.

"Yes," he said, nodding. His eyes were very tired. He
looked much older than he'd looked that afternoon—when
he'd been telling me about the good fishing at Sullivan's
Point. The blue of his eyes had been piercing then; it was
faded now. His Cupid's bow mouth had been animated
then; it now looked as if it had shot its last arrow.

"What is it, Colby?" he asked.

"I'd like to talk to you."

He nodded briefly. "Come in."

I followed him into the cabin. There wasn't much change
since I'd left it three hours earlier. Handy had probably
gone straight to bed the moment Ann and I cleared out. I
looked around the room quickly. The only thing that stuck
in my memory was the cigarette burning in an ash tray
near the telephone.

"I was asleep," he said. "What is it?"

"I didn't mean to wake you," I said.

"That's all right. What is it?"

"I want some policemen."

"Why?"

"It's complicated," I said.

"Life usually is," Handy replied, and he sighed a cu-
riously forlorn sigh. "Since you got me out of bed, why
don't you tell me about it?"

"My fiancée is missing," I said.

"What do you mean by that, exactly?" Handy asked.
He slipped the lid from the cut-glass cigarette box and
took a filter-tip cigarette which he immediately placed in
his mouth. "Cigarette?" he asked.

"No, thank you."

Handy fired the cigarette, using the lighter from the
table. "Now what's this about your fiancée being missing?" he asked. He blew out a long stream of smoke.
Some of the life seemed to be coming back into his eyes.
"Bad habit," he said. "Always take a cigarette when I
wake up."

"Yes," I said. "The girl—"

"Do you believe this stuff about throat cancer?" Handy asked.

"What?"

"Cigarettes," he said. "Causing throat cancer?"

"Oh. I don't know. I've never given it much thought."

"All the good things in life are either forbidden or no good for you," Handy said. He smiled tiredly. "That's not the way it goes. I quoted it wrong."

"We checked into a motel run by a man named Mike Barter," I said.

"Yes. At the Point."

"Yes. I left Ann in her cabin. She's gone now. Clothes, luggage, everything. Gone."

"*Who* did you leave in the cabin?" Handy asked.

"Ann. My fiancée."

"Oh," Handy said. He looked puzzled. He drew in on his cigarette slowly.

"The girl who was with me this afternoon," I explained.

Handy blew out another stream of smoke. "I don't think I follow you, Colby," he said thoughtfully.

"The girl who was with me," I said patiently. "When your trooper pulled us in. This afternoon. When he gave me the ticket."

Handy lifted his eyes to meet mine.

"*What* girl?" he asked.

"The girl—" I stopped dead. Our eyes were locked over the table. The Cupid's bow mouth was taut and drawn now. The blue eyes were wide awake and alert. Justice Oliver Handy was *en garde* and ready to start fencing.

"I don't remember any girl," he said. "Fred brought you in alone this afternoon."

"I see," I said.

Handy smiled. "Perhaps it was the long drive," he said.

"Or perhaps it was the telephone call," I answered.

"The what?"

"The call you undoubtedly received just before I got

here. The reason for the burning cigarette in that ash tray."
I gestured with my head. "What's going on, Handy?"

"I have no idea what you mean," Handy said.

"Don't you? You know goddamn well I had a girl with
me today. Now what's the pitch?"

"If there was a young lady with you, I didn't see her."

"She fell asleep right on your couch!" I shouted.

"I didn't see her!"

"What are you trying to pull? What's happening here?
Why the big coverup? Do you think you're going to—"

"I didn't see any girl," Handy said firmly.

"Okay, Handy." I got up. I pointed my finger under
his nose and said, "You may think this hick burg is the
beginning and the end of the world, but you've got your
geography figured a little wrong. There are state cops, and
there are federal cops, too—and kidnaping happens to be
a federal offense!"

"There's a state trooper who will testify that he arrested
you while you were alone," Handy said. "Why don't you
relax, Colby?"

"There are state troopers who'd shoot their own moth-
ers, too," I said. "I want some cops. Do I get them from
you, or do I have to start working?"

"Why do you want cops? To trace the disappearance of
a nonexistent girl?"

"No," I said. I grinned. "You don't think I'm crazy,
do you? You don't think I'd ask for police aid on something as obviously lunatic as that, do you? I want cops
because I found a pool of blood in a motel closet. I think
the cops might be interested in finding out who or what
made that blood."

"They might," Handy said.

"Well?"

"I'll call a trooper," he said. "I don't want to stand in
the way of a private citizen reporting a suspected crime."
He shrugged. "About the girl, though . . ." He shrugged
again.

"What girl?" I said.

Handy lifted his eyes, and a slight smile began forming

on his face. Slowly, methodically, he stubbed out his cigarette. "I'll call a trooper," he said, and he rose and walked to the telephone. The cigarette in the ash tray there had burned down to the filter tip and was beginning to smolder. Unceremoniously, Handy stubbed it out. He lifted the receiver and dialed four numbers.

"I have a theory about people," he said to me.

"Yeah?"

"Yes. I happen to believe that most of them are sensible. I'm also something of an optimist. I believe—" He cut himself short and said into the phone, "Hello, Fred? Did I get you up? Oh, well I'm sorry. No, nothing too important. Remember that young fellow you brought in this afternoon? Speeding. The detective, remember?" Handy paused. "No," he said emphatically, "he was *alone*. Nobody with him." Handy paused again, listening. "Yes, that's right. Yes, now you've got it. Well, he thinks he's run afoul of some trouble out at Mike Barter's place. Thought the local police might give him a hand. Think you can take a run over?" Handy listened. "No, not Mike's. I'm calling from my place. Sure. Okay then, we'll be expecting you. Listen, tell Janet I'm sorry about calling at this hour, will you? Fine."

He hung up.

"Be right over," he said. "Nice fellow, Fred."

"You were philosophizing a minute ago," I said.

"Oh, yes. People." Handy went to the cigarette box and lighted another cigarette. "Most of them are sensible, don't you think?"

"I suppose."

"Oh, yes," Handy said. "Yes. Most of them are sensible. Any man will eventually come to the realization that there's no sense in shoveling manure against the tide."

"Meaning?"

"Meaning it's sweeter-smelling and much less energetic to simply take a bench on the boardwalk, away from the breakers."

"Unless there happens to be something you want in the ocean," I said.

"It's been my experience, Colby, that there is absolutely nothing you can find in the ocean which you can't also find on the land."

"A lot of fish will be surprised to hear that."

"A lot of fish would be surprised to hear that anything but ocean exists at all. That's still no argument for shoveling against the tide."

"I don't know what you're talking about," I said. "If you've got something to say, say it in English."

"The English language," Handy said, "becomes a skill when you can use it and not make it sound like English."

"I thought the purpose of language was communication," I said. "If you're trying to communicate, your 'ocean' is away over my head."

"Very good," Handy said, smiling. "Very, very good."

"What are you trying to say?"

"I'm trying to tell you to relax. Stop shoveling. Show a little optimism." Handy paused. "This nonexistent girl friend of yours."

"Yes?"

"Relax, Colby."

"Why?"

"Optimism. Show a little optimism."

"You know she exists," I said.

"I know nothing. I'm simply asking you to look on the bright side. Let us suppose for an instant that she *does* exist. You came here to Sullivan's Point with her, you rented separate cabins, and now she's vanished. All assuming she existed in the first place."

"She existed," I said. "She does exist. Say what you've got to say."

"I'm saying that *if* she did exist, *if* she did indeed vanish . . . she's probably safe right now." Handy fixed me with a level stare. "And she probably will be safe when this is all over and done with."

"*Is* she safe now?" I asked.

Handy shrugged. "Your nonexistent friend? I would say that she is safe, yes. I would say that she is a lot safer than she could be were you to start . . . ah . . . shoveling manure against the tide.''

"We're back to the ocean again, huh?"

"The ocean is very peaceful. You don't know how nice it is not to live in a land-locked state."

"Where is she?" I said.

"I haven't the faintest idea," Handy said. He paused. "I never even saw her."

"But she's safe?"

"Colby, would you like some sound advice?"

"I'm listening."

"Yes, but your attitude is an arrogant one. I'm a lot older than you, and a lot wiser, and I've done a bit of shoveling in my day, too. I don't shovel any more. Take that antagonistic look off your face."

"Is that your advice?"

"My advice is this. Go back to the motel. Go to sleep. By tomorrow afternoon, all of this will be in the past. You can continue your vacation as if nothing happened."

"With or without Ann?"

"Who's Ann?"

"Will she be back by tomorrow afternoon? Safe?"

"I don't know who she is. But I have every reason to believe you could continue your vacation as planned."

"One other question, Your Honor," I said.

"Yes?"

"The person who bled in that closet. Will he or she be able to continue a vacation as planned?"

"In life, people bleed. You're a cop. You should know that. Some bleed. Some *have* to bleed."

"You're a very cryptic fellow, Your Honor," I said. "In our state, we don't happen to believe that some must bleed. We're idealists. We like to think that no one *has* to bleed. That's why we've got a police department."

"And this magnificent police department of yours has undoubtedly stopped the flow of blood, has it?"

"We try," I said.

"Colby," Handy said, "don't be a goddamn hero."

"What?"

"Go back to your cabin and sleep this off. Tomorrow, pack up and go on your way. This is friendly advice. Ride with the punches. Think whatever the hell you want to think. Think at night. In the daytime, play the cop, or the butcher, or the homey j.p., or whatever particular role life has doled out to you. Don't think during the daytime. If you start thinking, you get in trouble. Just play your part, Colby. Save your thinking for when you're alone—and never think out loud."

"You're thinking out loud right now," I said.

"Only because I'm trying to save you a lot of trouble."

"Thanks," I said. "I appreciate it."

"You don't. Your tone of voice tells me you don't." Handy sighed. "Fred should be here soon. When he comes, I suggest you tell him you were mistaken about that blood. That's my strong advice to you."

"I wasn't mistaken," I paused. "I don't make mistakes about blood."

Handy sighed again. "You can be making a bigger mistake," he said. "A bigger mistake than you imagine."

And that's when the knock sounded on the door.

8

IT WAS AMAZING TO WATCH THE CHANGE THAT CAME OVER Handy as he opened the door. A few minutes before he admitted Fred, he was something of the melancholy cynic. He'd been thinking aloud, but he stopped thinking the second his hand pulled open the door. He stopped thinking, and he became the small town j.p. again. His stature changed, his voice changed, his speech pattern changed.

"Well, well," he said. "Fred. Come in, come in. Heck of a time to be gallivantin' over the countryside, isn't it? Come in, come in."

"I was sound asleep," Fred said. He looked over at me briefly. He was wearing his trooper's uniform, but he needed a shave and he looked a little seedy. "What's the trouble?"

"Young fellow here thinks he saw blood in one of Mike Barter's cabins." Handy paused and turned to me. "Or is that right?" he asked in a last stab at getting me to forget what I'd seen.

"That's right," I said.

"Probably somebody cut himself shaving," Fred said.

"I doubt it. People don't shave in closets, and no shaving cut makes a puddle on the floor."

" 'Course, it's something to look into," Handy said.

"Sure," Fred answered. "Why don't we get started?"

"Well, you won't be needing me," Handy said. "You know your job, Fred."

"Sure," Fred said. "You get back to bed."

"Fred'll take good care of you," Handy said, and he led us to the door. We walked out into the night. It was

63

getting on toward five o'clock, and there was that expectant hush on the air, that silence that comes just before false dawn. Every sound seemed to be magnified. The crunch of Fred's boots on the path, the quiet snick of the door when Handy eased it shut, the whisper of wind in the pines surrounding the log cabin.

"No motorcycle this morning?" I asked.

"Took my own car," Fred said.

His own car was a buick station wagon. We walked to it quickly. There was a big meadow behind the log cabin, and the mist was rising from it. We got in, and Fred started the car and then backed out onto the highway. We drove silently. Around us, the morning was beginning to unfold, the sky in the east paling, the stars beginning to desert the vault of night.

"Blood, huh?" Fred said.

"Yes."

"Well."

"Lots of it."

"Mmm."

"In a closet."

"No body?"

"No."

"Mmmmm."

"There's another thing," I said.

"What?"

"I checked in with a girl. She's gone."

"Mmmm?"

"Yes. The girl I was with when you picked me up yesterday."

Fred didn't take his eyes from the road.

"I don't remember any girl," he said.

"I didn't think you would."

"Then why'd you mention it?"

"I just wanted to make sure you got your instructions."

"I don't know what you're talking about."

"Nobody does."

"We're just small town hicks," Fred said sarcastically. "We don't understand city folk."

"We use big words."

"Yeah," Fred said.

"I've got a small word for you," I said.

"Yeah?"

"Yeah. Kidnap."

"That's a good word. Even we hicks heard of it."

"I've got a slightly bigger one. Want to hear it?"

"Not if it's too big."

"You be the judge. Homicide."

"Homicide is pretty big." Fred paused. "Want some advice?"

"Everybody else is giving it out."

"Those words. Tongue-twisters. I wouldn't use them too often if I was you."

"Why not?"

"We hicks might not understand them. We hicks might think you was trying to show off."

"Do you think I'm trying to show off, Fred?"

"Me? Hell, I'm a cop, too. I have only respect for fellow cops. Especially big city detectives."

"You can still get out of this, you know."

"Get out of what?"

"Whatever you're in, Fred."

"I'm in a Buick station wagon," he answered. "That's all I'm in."

"How about that blood?"

"How about it? Assuming there is any, lots of things can make a puddle of blood." He paused. "Barter runs a clean place."

"Does he?"

"Cleanest in the state."

"What's the monthly rake-off there?"

"The what? The what?"

"The rake-off. For looking the other way in case Barter gets dirty."

"Barter don't get dirty. He runs a family-type establishment. He's a married man himself, don't you know that? Nossir, he runs a clean place." Fred turned to me briefly. "Besides, the cops in this state don't take graft."

"There isn't a cop in the world who takes graft," I agreed. "Only you're talking to a cop, remember?"

"Okay, maybe a speeding ticket once in a while. Save the guy the trouble of appearing, take the fine right on the highway. That's a different story. But nothing big. You can't fix anything in this state. This state is as square as they come."

"Sure."

"That's no bull. It ain't like your city. Your city, you can fix anything. Assault, rape, even murder. Not here. We got a D.A. with a thousand eyes. Commissions all over the place. Him and the State's Attorney. Ike and Mike. Big crime fighters."

We were on the road to the Point now. The sun was intimidating the sky, and the sky blushed a pale orange. It was going to be another beautiful day.

"So if there's blood, maybe there's blood," Fred said. "But maybe you saw wrong. Maybe the blood is your imagination, you know? Like the broad you claim was with you."

"Do you know a girl named Blanche?" I asked.

"No."

"Guy named Joe Carlisle?"

"Nope."

"Girl named Stephanie?"

Fred paused a moment. "Stephanie what?" he asked.

"Stephanie Carlisle. Joe's wife."

"Oh. No, I don't. No."

"Who *do* you know named Stephanie?"

"Oh. Kid I went to high school with. Haven't seen her in years."

"What did Ann see?" I asked suddenly.

"Ann?" Fred said, stepping around my very subtle trap. "Who's Ann?"

"Forget it," I said, and we drove the rest of the way to the Point in silence. The motel site was shrouded with mist when we arrived. Mist clung to the ground and to the tall pines. Mist hung over the lake and nestled in the canoes loaded upside down on the lakefront racks. Mist swirled up around the cabins, white cabins with shuttered windows, the shutters done in pastel blues and greens. The Cadillac was still parked in front of the office. The license plate read:

$$\boxed{\text{SB-1412}}$$

"That's Carlisle's car," I said to Fred. "Recognize it?"

"Nope," he answered.

"Lots of Caddies in the area, I suppose."

"We got our share."

"And all with veep license tags, I guess."

"If you can afford a Caddy, you can afford the veep plate. You can get the state to print the word 'SHIT' on it, if you like. It just costs you an extra ten bucks when you register the vehicle."

"Why do you suppose a man named Joseph Carlisle would put the initials SB on his license plate?"

"That's Joseph Carlisle's business," Fred said. "I make it a practice of keeping my nose out of other people's business."

"That's a healthy attitude for a cop, all right," I said, and we got out of the car and walked to the office.

Fred pulled off his right glove and rapped on the door. From somewhere inside the cabin, I could hear music. The light was on, as if Barter were expecting company. Everyone was expecting company. This was the ideal time of day for guests dropping in, and so everyone in Sullivan's Corners and at Sullivan's Point was prepared for the eventuality.

The door opened.

Barter had shaving cream on his face, and a straight-edged razor in his right hand. I looked past him into the office. The inner door, the one hiding the apartment at the back, was closed.

"Hello, Fred," Barter said.

"Mr. Barter," Fred acknowledged, using a formality which sounded completely false. I listened to the music.

It was coming from behind the closed door. It whispered into the cabin on a sprinkle of piano notes, the theme from "Picnic," coupled with "Moonglow."

"Tell you all about his missing girl?" Barter asked.

"Yep."

"All about the bloody mess in cabin eleven?"

"Yep."

"Did you give him the drunk test?" Barter asked.

Fred grinned. "Doesn't seem to me he's polluted, Mr. Barter."

"Just temporarily insane, maybe," Barter said, and he returned Fred's grin. "Happens sometimes. The country air. Infects a man."

"Could we look at the cabin, Mr. Barter?" Fred said.

"Sure," Barter answered. "Just let me wash off this shaving cream." He smiled, and unnecessarily added, "I was just shaving when you came."

He went to the apartment door and opened it. Part of the long couch was visible when the door opened. There was a woman on the couch, or rather a pair of woman's legs because that was all of her that could be seen. Clean, tapering legs, one stretched against the couch, the other bent at the knee so that together they formed a triangle of flesh and bone. The door closed.

"Mrs. Barter," Fred said. "Pretty woman."

"How could you tell?" I said.

"That she's pretty? Hell . . ."

"No. That she was Mrs. Barter. All *I* saw was legs."

Fred shrugged. "Who else would be in Mike Barter's apartment?"

"That's praiseworthy logic," I said.

"Look," Fred said, "if you had a wife who looked like Mike's wife does, there wouldn't be nobody else in that room. You don't have to be a big city cop to figure that one."

"Never having met Mrs. Barter—"

"Take my word for it," Fred said emphatically, closing the conversation. He paused a moment, and then reopened it with remarkable versatility. "Take my word for it," he said.

We waited.

There was an air of unreality about the room. Early morning is an intimate time of day. You don't stand around with strangers at 5:15 A.M. You talk with friends who've come to pick you up for a fishing trip. You smoke a cigarette with your wife in a warm bed with rumpled sheets and you watch the dawn come up. You share a cup of coffee while the kids fidget at the kitchen table waiting to start on the long-promised vacation. You stand in a doorway, and you kiss your girl good morning after the senior prom. Or you meet the fellows in the local all-night hamburger joint, and you talk about last night's escapades, and you laugh a little, and you share the morning with them because they are your friends. Early morning was never intended for strangers. You do not start a new day with a stranger.

I was starting a new day with a stranger.

He leaned against Mike Barter's desk, and he idly tweaked his nose. Then he stared at his thumb and forefinger. Then he said, "There's oil on the nose, did you know that? You can put a nice polish on a pipe by first rubbing your nose flaps and then rubbing the briar. Lots of people don't know that."

I was tired. I hadn't slept since seven-thirty yesterday morning. I didn't want to hear about nose flaps from a state trooper named Fred. I didn't smoke a pipe. I wouldn't have cared if my own nose contained enough oil to warrant a derrick which would bring me four millions dollars a year. There was only one person I wanted to be with, only one person whose hand I wanted to take when the sun came up. I didn't know where that person was.

Someone in the back rooms dropped the record player arm. Music invaded the cabin again. The arm was lifted and then dropped in its proper groove at the beginning of the record. There were a few whispered syllables, the intimate conversation of needle and groove before the waxed impressions were captured. And then the record started.

Frank Sinatra. At 5:15 A.M. At least there was one old
friend in the room.

"He don't sing so hot," Fred said.

"I like him." I was beginning to feel that hypertension
that comes with no sleep and too much pressure. If Fred
had said another word about the merits of my old friend
Frank Sinatra's voice, I would have punched him right in
the nose. I'd grown up with Sinatra's voice. Sure, I'd kid-
ded the girls who'd swooned and screamed, but under-
neath I'd always liked him. He was a part of my youth and
a part of my adolescence, and he seemed like the only
sane thing in the world right now, the only sure thing I
could count on. I waited for Fred to say more. I unconsciously clenched my right fist.

"I like Elvis Presley," he said.

"What do you suppose is keeping Barter?" I asked.

"Wiping his face," Fred said. "Elvis Presley's got
style."

"What takes a man so damn long to wipe off a little
shaving cream?"

"You're jumpy," Fred said. "You got to learn to take
life in stride." He paused. "A distinctive style. That's
what the disc jockeys say. Minute the record begins, you
know it's Presley."

The door opened. The legs flashed into view again, and
then the closing door screened them. They were good legs.
Barter smiled.

"You like Elvis Presley?" Fred said.

"That fellow with the guitar?" Barter asked.

"Yeah, him."

"He's good," Barter agreed, nodding. He had wiped
the shaving cream from his face. There was a streak of
clean skin across the beard stubble, the area he'd shaved
before we arrived. It looked like a wide white scar. "You
fellows care for a cup of coffee?" Barter asked.

"No," I said quickly.

"I might go for a cup of coffee," Fred said.

"No damn coffee," I said. "Let's get over to that
cabin."

"He's jumpy," Fred said.

"Can't blame him," Barter answered. "Been up all night. I'm a little jumpy myself."

"Well, might as well see that blood," Fred said. "We can always have the coffee later."

"Let's go, let's go," I said impatiently.

"Got to get the keys," Barter said. He went to a peg on the wall and took down the ring of keys. "Okay."

He went out of the office. Sinatra was still singing. Occasionally, a woman's voice picked up snatches of the song and then let it die in a hum. The voice was low and throaty. If it belonged to the legs, they made a lethal combination. The sun was climbing. The lake was still and serene. I was the last man on earth, and I was walking across a beautiful stage set with professional actors who knew their parts while I had forgotten all my lines.

"Personally," Fred said, "I liked it when he gyrated. Showed he had rhythm. I like a singer with rhythm."

"Como's good," Barter said. "He's very casual."

"So's Bing Crosby," Fred said. "You can't beat him for being casual."

"I think Como's more casual," Barter said.

"That's the hardest thing in the world to do," Fred said. "Appear casual, I mean. Think of the pressure those guys are under. Yet they manage to look casual."

"It's a hard thing, all right," Barter said. "You've got to respect them for it."

"Why don't you start a goddamn fan club?" I snapped.

Fred chuckled. "He's jumpy," he said.

"Say that one more time, trooper!" I warned.

"There's the cabin he says the blood was in," Barter interrupted.

Fred wouldn't be interrupted. "City cops are tough, ain't they?" he said to me.

"Yeah," I said, my voice rising, "city cops are tough! Now how about that!"

"How about it?" Fred said mildly.

"How about it?" I said. *"How about it?"*

"Come on, fellers," Barter said placatingly. "Come on now."

He climbed the steps to eleven and inserted the key in the lock. I glared at Fred. Fred grinned at me. Barter threw open the door.

"Right in here," he said.

Almost before he entered the cabin, Fred said, "I don't see no blood."

"In the closet," I said.

"Where's that?"

"Over here," Barter said. He threw open the closet door. Fred walked over to it. I waited.

"No blood in here," Fred said.

"What do you—?"

"Take a look for yourself."

I went to the closet. There was a square of linoleum tacked to the floor, tacked *securely* to the floor, tacked to fit exactly the floor of the closet. The closet smelled of soap.

"Rip up the linoleum," I said.

"What for?"

"You'll find a scrubbed floor. But you can't scrub all the blood out of wood. Rip up the linoleum."

"You know I can't do that," Fred said. "How can I destroy another man's property? For Pete's sake, you're a cop. You know I can't—"

"I'm a cop, and I know what you can do and what you can't do, and I also know it doesn't make any difference when you really *want* to do something. I'm telling you there's blood under that linoleum. You going to rip it up, or do I have to go over your head?"

"Over my head how?" Fred asked.

"Other cops. Goddamnit, there are other cops in this state! I'll go to your crusading D.A., or even to your State's Attorney! Now how about it?"

"No," Fred said.

"Okay, pal," I said. "Let's end this farce right now." I started out of the cabin. Fred stepped into my path.

"Which farce are you talking about?"

"My missing girl, and this blood, and the runaround I've been getting from every damn tinhorn I've contacted. What the hell are you running here? A little dictatorship? Okay. We'll see how the D.A. feels about kidnap and possible homicide. We'll see how he—"

"Lower your voice," Fred said.

"Don't tell me what to do, pal. I'll talk as—"

"I'll tell you once more. Lower your voice."

"And I'll tell you once more. I'll—"

Fred grabbed my arm. "You'd better come along with me," he said.

"What!"

"Disorderly conduct. Disturbing the peace."

"What!" I said again. I shook his hand off my arm, and I took a step backwards, balling my fists.

"If you want to add assault to it, start swinging," Fred said.

I was ready to do just that when he yanked the .38 Police Special from the holster at his side.

"That's a good boy," he said, and he grinned, and Barter winked at him.

9

Lots of small towns don't have jails.

Sullivan's Corners had one.

There was a wino in the cell with me. He was asleep with his mouth open when Fred brought me in. When the door clanked shut, the wino sat bolt upright, blinked his eyes, and then stared at me.

"What'd you do?" he asked.

"Nothing. Go to sleep."

"You got a hair across?"

"Yes. Go to sleep."

"I'm only trying to be friendly."

"I committed an ax murder," I said. "I killed my wife and our fourteen children."

"Yeah?" he said, impressed. "What was the matter? She nag you?"

"She was having an affair with a police dog," I said.

The wino blinked. "You can't trust German shepherds," he said at last. "Collies are good dogs." He blinked again. "Gee, it's morning, ain't it?"

"Yes," I said. "I'm going to sleep."

"You want this lower, I'll be happy to change."

"I'll take the upper." I gripped the edge of the double-decker bunk and swung myself up.

"Lots of guys don't like uppers," the wino said. "I got to hand it to you. Commit a couple of murders, and then go right to sleep afterwards."

"I need my strength," I told him.

"Why?"

"Because sooner or later, they'll have to let me out of

this place. And when they do . . ." I let the sentence trail. The wino was silent for a long time. The early morning sunlight filtered through the small barred window. I was almost asleep when the wino said, "Why'd you choose an ax?"

"Huh?"

"An ax. Why'd you pick that?"

"Because Fred has both my guns," I mumbled, and I drifted off.

I never dream.

Psychiatrists say you always dream; you just don't remember the dreams when you wake up. Okay, I always dream but I never remember the dreams when I wake up. If a tree falls in a forest and nobody's there to see it, did it fall?

I never dream.

I sleep, and I wake up. Usually, I get dressed and go to work. If it's my day off, I hand around and have a leisurely cup of coffee, and then maybe I'll read the paper or call Ann, or listen to some records. That's my life. Dull. I usually wake up in the same room. My bedroom at the house where I board. It's a nice room. There are ships on the wallpaper design and sometimes they make me seasick, but it's a nice room. The radiators clang in the winter time, but I like a clanging radiator. It makes me feel as if it's working.

I was not working.

I was on vacation.

I woke up, and I hadn't dreamed, and there were no ships sailing across the walls. It's a strange feeling to come out of a deep sleep and have no idea at all where you are. I looked at the ceiling, and I looked at the walls, and it took me a few moments to remember I was in jail.

I looked at my watch. It was one-thirty.

"You're a late sleeper," a voice said.

I looked across the cell. The man opposite me, sitting on the bench, wore soiled dungarees and a tee shirt. He hadn't shaved since the Smith Brothers invented cough drops. His nose was red, and his eyes were red, and his lips were parched. He was my wino.

"Good morning," I said.

"Good *afternoon,*" he corrected.

"What's for breakfast?" I asked.

"Breakfast has come and gone."

"What's for lunch?"

"You missed that, too."

"Has there been any word from the governor?" I said.

"What?"

"Never mind." I swung my legs over the side of the bunk. "Who's in charge of this place?"

"Feller named Tex Planett. He ain't really from Texas. They call him Tex 'cause he's kind of long and rangy." The wino paused. "Also because he's the sheriff of Sullivan's Corners. You know, like who expects to find a sheriff, except out West?" The wino shrugged. "Tex."

"You're pretty familiar with the local law, huh?"

"I'm in and out of this place regularly," the wino said. And then, offhandedly, "I'm a vagrant. M'name's Tuckem."

"Mine's Colby."

"Please to make your acquaintance," Tuckem said. He paused again. "I drink."

"Okay," I said.

"I ain't getting your permission; I'm only stating a fact. I been drinking for twenty years straight now. It's a miracle I ain't got a wet brain. Someday I'm going to write my autobiography, like this *I'll Cry Tomorrow* thing, you know? I got the title all picked out."

"Yeah."

"Yeah. You want to hear it?"

"Sure," I said.

"It's all about me, you understand," Tuckem said. "An autobiography. Also, it will contain my philosophy of life. You want to hear the title?"

"Sure," I said again.

Tuckem spread his hands grandly. *Tuckem All,*" he said. He grinned. "You like it?"

"It's good."

"You ought to write one. Feller who commits ax murders sure ought to write a book."

"My uncle wrote one," I said.

"Yeah? Was he an ax murderer, too?"

"No. He burned his victims to death. Didn't you read his book?"

"Which one is that?" Tuckem asked.

"Flesh in the Pan," I said.

"I missed that one," Tuckem said seriously. "I read one by a kidnaper, though. You read that one?"

"Which one?" I said.

"It was called *Snatch.* Very interesting." This time, Tuckem smiled. I smiled with him. "You didn't really commit no ax murder, did you?"

"No."

"I didn't think so. Why're you in here?"

"I know too much."

"That's why almost everybody I know's in jail. They either know too much, or they don't know enough."

"What's the local law consist of?"

"Well, there's Tex. He's sheriff. He's got four deputies, I think. Yep, four. That's it."

"What about state troopers?"

"One, so far as I know. Feller named Fred."

"What about Handy?"

"He's the j.p. Harmless guy. Used to be a fighter, that man. I can remember when he used to be a fighter. No more now. No spunk."

We heard footsteps in the corridor. Tuckem looked up. I turned toward the barred door. The man who came into view was tall and thin. He had cool blue eyes and a crew cut. A star was on his chest, and he carried a .45 in a holster at his side.

"Hope I'm not breaking anything up," he said.

"Tex?" I said.

"That's me." He paused. "The real name's Salvatore. Salvatore Planetti. It got shortened to Tex Planett. That's 'cause I'm a pioneer." He looked me over. "Understand you were raising a bit of a ruckus this morning, Colby."

"Was I?"

"According to Fred. I just wanted you to know the local law ain't asleep around here."

"Isn't it?"

"No sir. I sent a deputy out to Mike Barter's place. Just checking, you understand. Had him look at Mike's register. Well, you was registered, all right, but you checked in alone. There wasn't no girl who signed the register with you."

"I could have told you that," I said.

"Well, I wanted to find out for myself." Planett cleared his throat. "My deputy also ripped up that linoleum in the closet."

"Did he?"

"I said he did, didn't I? Don't you believe me?"

"Sure. I believe you. What'd he find?"

"Nothing."

"That's what I figured you'd say he found."

"You don't believe me, huh?"

"Tex," I said, "Salvatore, as long as I'm on this side of the bars, I'd believe you if you said the world was round."

"Well, it is," Tex said.

"And I believe you. See?"

"Dis cond's only a misdemeanor. So's disturbing the peace. Ten dollar fine, and away you go," Tex said.

"This makes twenty so far," I said. "Can I deduct it?"

"What?"

"When do you get the ten? Before or after the cell is unlocked?"

"You can come with me to the front office," Tex said. "Pay me there." He unlocked the door. "Hello, Tuckem," he said belatedly.

"When do I get out?" Tuckem wanted to know.

"You sober?"

"Sure."

"Cool off a little while," Tex said.

I stepped out of the cell. Tex closed and locked the door again. "This way," he said, and I followed him down the long stone corridor. He unlocked another door at the end of the corridor, and then led me into an office with a desk, some filing cabinets, a water cooler, and a rack full of rifles.

"You've got a nice cell block," I said.

"We figure if you've got a big enough jail, you don't need half as big a police force."

"Does it work?"

"The jail or the police force?"

"The philosophy."

"Sure. Give me the ten bucks, and I'll give you a receipt."

I took out my wallet. Tex was already writing the receipt. I handed him the sawbuck. "What's the first name?" he asked.

"Philip."

He put down the pen, tore off the receipt with its two carbons, and handed me one of the carbon copies. "Here you go."

"You're forgetting something, aren't you?"

"What's that?"

"I checked in with two guns."

"I never saw them," Tex said.

"Fred took them from me."

"Then see Fred about them. I hope you got licenses for the guns, otherwise you'll be right back in here again."

"Where do I find Fred?"

"He's likely to be anywhere." Tex rose. "Well, so long, Colby. Been nice having you."

"Send me your literature," I said, and I walked out.

The town was busy. It was busy with a small town's hustle and bustle. And, as always with a stranger in a small town, I watched the people and wondered where they were going in such a hurry. I was hungry. I hadn't eaten since the afternoon before. Food seemed to me, at that moment, the most important thing in the world. There was also a phone call I had to make because I needed help. I picked out a small coffee pot, walked in, ordered three hamburgers, a cup of coffee, and a piece of chocolate cream pie, and then I went to the phone booth and deposited a dime. I dialed the operator.

When she came on, I said, "Long distance, please."

I waited.

Another voice said, "Long *dis*-tance."

"I'm calling Argyle 4-3187."

"Thank you." I heard a lot of clicking, and behind the clicking the hum of a lot of operators doing their work. Then my operator said, "Fifty-five cents for the first three minutes, please."

I deposited the change.

"What is the number you're calling from, sir?"

"I read it from the dial plate.

"Thank you," she said, and then I listened while she began ringing.

The phone was lifted on the other end.

"Twenty-third Precinct, Sergeant Colombo."

"Al," I said, "this is Phil Colby. Is the lieutenant in?"

"Yeah, just a second, Phil." Colombo did a vocal doubletake. "Hey, I thought you were on vacation."

"I am. Get him, please."

"Sure."

I waited.

"DeMorra here," a voice said.

"Lieutenant, this is Phil Colby."

"Who?"

"Phil . . ."

"Oh, yes, yes. What is it, Phil?"

"I'm in trouble, sir," I said.

"That business with the car? O'Hare explained it to me."

"No, sir. Not that. My fiancée's gone."

"What do you mean, gone?"

"Missing, sir. Taken from her cabin."

DeMorra was silent for several moments. "Are you sure, Colby?"

"Yes, sir."

"Have you gone to the local police?"

"Yes, sir. They claim she never was."

"Never was? What do you mean?"

"Sir, I don't know what's going on here, but there are a lot of people in it, and they're all lying their fool heads off. There's also a puddle of blood in one of the cabins at the motel, and the locals are ready to write it off as a figment of my imagination. I spent the morning in jail, sir, and Ann's still missing, and I frankly don't—"

"In jail?"

". . . know what to do next."

"Where are you, Colby?"

"In a phone booth."

"Where?"

"A restaurant in Sullivan's Corners, sir. They just let me out of jail."

"Isn't it possible your girl just decided to pick up and go?"

"She was sound asleep the last time I saw her, sir. Also, she doesn't have her own car with her or anything like that. Besides, there was no reason for her to . . ."

"You never can tell with women," DeMorra said.

"Sir, if that were the case, there'd be no reason for all these people to lie about her being there in the first place, don't you see?"

"Yes," DeMorra said thoughtfully.

"Sir?"

"Yes?"

"I . . . I need help."

"Yes, I can see that. What's the number there?" I read it to him from the dial plate. "Will you be there a while?"

"I just ordered some lunch. I haven't eaten since—"

"All right, let me see what I can do. I'll call you back in about ten minutes."

"Yes, sir. I appreciate it."

"All right, Colby. Let me get to work," and he hung up.

I went out of the phone booth and over to my table. The hamburgers and coffee were waiting. I was sitting down when the door to the restaurant opened.

A girl I knew was standing in the doorframe.

10

SHE WAS WEARING THE SAME PURPLE SILK DRESS SHE'D worn the last time I'd seen her. Her face was made up again. Her eyes, despite the make-up, were tired, very tired. She carried a long white stole over her arm.

"Blanche!" I said, and she turned quickly, spotted me, and for a minute seemed about to leave. She apparently changed her mind, held her ground, and waited as I approached her.

"Hello, Blanche," I said.

She looked up at me suspiciously. "I don't think I know you," she said.

I wasn't prepared for that. I stared at her and then said, "Does it matter?"

"Maybe not. What do you want?"

"I want to buy you a cup of coffee."

"What's the special occasion?"

"Do I have to be in love to buy you a cup of coffee?"

"Not necessarily."

"Okay, then."

"Okay. But I'm in a hurry."

"So am I. Come on over."

We walked to the table. Blanche sat, and the man behind the counter said, "Hello, Blanche." She nodded at him.

"Another cup of coffee," I said to the counterman. "For the lady."

The "lady" bit killed him. His eyebrows shot up onto his forehead, and then he turned to draw the coffee.

"Where'd you disappear to last night?" I asked.

"I don't know what you're talking about."

"We both know what I'm talking about," I said.

"Mister, all I want's a cup of coffee."

"That's all you'll get."

"Good."

"But you won't mind if I ask some questions?"

"I *will* mind."

"Why?"

"I don't like questions."

"Do I have to get tough?"

"It'd get you no place. Men don't scare me. I've had men up to here."

"My father used to say, 'Treat a lady like a whore, and a whore like a lady.' How do I treat you, Blanche?"

She raised her eyes and looked at me long and hard. "Like a lady," she answered. Her voice was very small.

"All right. I need help."

"Why come to me?"

"Because I think you know what happened last night."

"I know nothing."

The counterman brought the coffee. "Anything else?" he asked.

"Nothing, thanks," I said. I bit into the hamburger. The counterman went back to his counter. Unconsciously, I whispered the next. "What happened, Blanche?"

Blanche answered my whisper with her own. "I don't know."

"What were you doing at Barter's place?"

"Nothing."

"Do you work there?"

"No."

"Do you?"

"No."

"Then what were you doing there?"

"I took a cabin."

"Alone?"

"Yes."

"Why?"

"I was sleepy."

"Who was the man in the wolves'-heads shorts?"

Blanche looked up sharply. "How . . . how did you . . . ?"

"I met him." I bit off another chunk of beef. "Were you with him before you came to my cabin?"

Blanche nodded.

"You were?"

"Yes."

"Why'd you come to me?"

"I . . . Mike asked me to."

"Why?"

"I don't know."

"How did he ask you to?"

"He just said . . . I should go to your cabin. He said I should . . ." Blanche paused. "Listen, I can get in trouble. Listen, I can't tell you any more."

"I thought men didn't scare you."

"They don't! I'm not afraid of Mike!"

"Who then?"

"I . . . I can't tell you any more."

"Did he ask you to keep me in the cabin? To keep me busy?"

Blanche bit her lip. "Y . . . yes."

"For how long?"

"Half-hour, an hour. I don't remember."

"Why?"

"I don't know."

"He must have given you a reason!"

"He didn't! I don't ask questions. I just do what I'm told."

"Then you do work for him?"

Blanche paused. "All right. I work for him."

"The other girls, too?"

"What other girls?"

"The ones scattered all over the motel. The 'wives' in the husband-and-wife teams I met."

"I don't know who you met. I suppose so."

"Who's Joe Carlisle?"

"Who?"

"Joe Carlisle. He's from Davistown."

"Oh. He's nothing."

"What do you mean?"

"He comes around now and then, does handy work for Mike. Mike pays him by . . . by . . . you know. Hez is the real handy man, though." She looked up into my face. "Hezekiah Hawkins. He lives near the motel, out at the Point. Got his own place on South Hunter Road."

"What about his wife?"

Fear darted momentarily into Blanche's eyes. "Who . . . whose wife?" she asked.

"Carlisle's."

"He's not married."

"There was a blonde with him last night. In the cabin my girl originally had. Her name is Stephanie. Do you know her?"

"No," Blanche said quickly.

"Did you see anyone enter my girl's cabin?"

"What girl?" Blanche said.

"Listen . . ."

"I didn't see any girl."

We stared at each other across the miles of tablecloth.

"What made the blood in cabin eleven?" I asked.

"What blood? I didn't see any blood."

"End of interview?" I asked.

"End of interview. I don't want trouble. There was enough trouble last night. Enough to last me a lifetime."

"What kind of trouble?"

"I don't know. Screaming and yelling and cars. I don't know."

"Screaming from where?"

"Some place in the motel."

"*Where* in the motel?"

"I don't know."

"*Where, Blanche?*"

"Cabin . . . cabin number eleven."

"Who was in that cabin?"

"I don't know."

"Think."

"I don't know."

"You do, Blanche. It's in your eyes. You do know."

"I can't tell you any more." Her eyes were pleading with me now. The phone in the booth began ringing. I shoved back my chair. Blanche reached for my hand suddenly. I turned to her.

"Your girl," she said. "She's . . . she's safe."

"What?" The phone kept ringing. The counterman came from behind the counter and headed for it. Quickly, I moved into the booth and lifted the receiver.

"Hello?"

"Colby, this is Lieutenant DeMorra."

"Yes, sir."

"Any new developments?"

"Just that I think Ann is safe, sir. I don't know how long she will be, though."

"All right. I'm sending Tony."

"Mitchell?"

"Yes. You know this is highly irregular, Colby, and you know it has to be unofficial. We don't want out-of-state police coming down on our necks with protests. I'm giving Tony sick leave. He's coming on his own. Where can he meet you?"

"How about right here?"

"What's the name of the place?"

"I don't know. It's the coffee pot right alongside the only bank in town."

"All right. He's starting now. Give him three or four hours. Make it six sharp, all right?"

"Fine." I paused. "Sir, my gun was taken from me."

"Tony'll bring you one." DeMorra paused. "Why? Do you think you'll need it?"

"I might."

"All right. Good luck, Colby."

"Thank you, sir."

I hung up.

When I walked out of the booth, Blanche was gone.

11

THERE WAS NO SENSE IN TAKING OFF AFTER BLANCHE. Even if I'd have found her, she'd done all the talking she was going to do. I sat down at the table and knocked off the remaining two hamburgers. When the counterman saw I'd finished the main course, he brought me my chocolate cream pie.

I was beginning to feel a little better. I'm the kind of fellow who likes to eat. You know, there are those who eat to live, and those who live to eat. I'm not exactly a live-to-eater, but I do like food. Also, when I've gone for any amount of time without stuffing something into my mouth, I get so I can't even think too straight. I was beginning to think a little straighter, or at least as straight as I'd ever thought. And I had to admit that things looked a little better. Ann was safe. Or at any rate Blanche had said so. Mitchell was on his way, and there wasn't a better cop in the 23rd. There were also a few other things I now knew which, while not entirely clearing up the picture, at least helped in that direction.

For one, there had been trouble in cabin 11 last night. Blanche had heard yelling and screaming and cars. Maybe the blood was a result of that trouble.

For another, I was fairly certain that no matter what else Mike Barter ran, he also ran a good-sized brothel.

That didn't put me any closer to finding Ann.

I paid my check and then went out to the street. I figured I'd better head back to Barter's motel if for no other reason than to pick up my bag and my car. I didn't know what ideas Mitchell would have when he arrived, but I wanted to be ready for whatever he suggested. Even if he didn't have an idea in his head, I felt a lot better just knowing he was on his way.

I caught a cab outside the bank and told the driver I wanted to go to Mike Barter's motel.

"At the Point?" he said.

"Yes."

"Got to give you a flat rate on that."

"What's the rate?"

"Two bucks," he said.

"That sounds appropriate."

We drove out to the motel. The Caddy with the SB license tag was still in front of the office. A little Ford was parked alongside it. Barter was nowhere in sight. My own car was parked just a little to the right of and behind the Ford. I got out of the cab and went straight to cabin 12. I wasn't surprised to find that the bloodstain along the wall had been scrubbed clean. I changed my clothes, packed whatever was hanging around, and then carried my bag to the car. As I passed the office, I heard voices. I stoppped.

It's impolite to eavesdrop unless you're a cop.

"I know she's here," a man's voice said, "so don't give me any of that crap."

The voice that answered him was low and throaty. "I prefer not to listen to profanity," it said. "If you're going to start swearing, you can leave right now."

"Where's Lois? That's all I want to know," the man said.

"And I told you. She left. This morning."

"Where'd she go?"

"To the railroad station. She said she was going back home."

"How come she didn't tell me anything about it?"

I could almost hear the woman shrugging. "How would I know? She made up her mind suddenly. She said she was leaving, and she left."

"Did she leave alone?"

"No. I drove her in with one of the other girls. Walked her to the station, in fact."

"What was she wearing?"

"A white dress," the woman said.

"This was at the railroad station in Sullivan's Corners?"

"Yes."

"I'm going to check there," the man said.

"Go ahead, check. We stopped for coffee in town, too. At The Green Door. You can check there, too."

"I will. You can damn well bet I will."

"You have a foul mouth," the woman said.

"I'm leaving. Your story better be right, or I'll be back."

The woman started to say something else, but I took off then and went to O'Hare's car. I opened the trunk and threw the bag in. Then I got behind the wheel, backed out of the court, and headed up the road. I pulled into the first cutoff I came to, and I killed the engine, and then I waited.

The Ford came along in about five minutes. I started the car and took off after it. If the driver knew about the twenty-five-mile speed limit, he didn't give a damn. He took the road's bumps as if he were testing Goodyear rubber. I had a lot of respect for O'Hare and his Chevvy, but I didn't want to lose this guy, so I tested the tires too. We both rumbled into Sullivan's Corners, and my young friend went straight to the railroad station. I got out of the car, went into the station to buy a magazine from the stand there, and watched him while he talked to the ticket seller.

He couldn't have been more than twenty-nine, sort of short, but packed with muscle that came from hard manual labor. His hair was a bright red. He wore dark gray trousers and a white shirt, the sleeves rolled up to the biceps. I paid for my magazine, and then went out to sit in the car. In a few moments, the redhead came out and piled into his Ford. He drove straight through the middle of town and then abruptly pulled to the curb. I didn't have to pull in behind him. I cruised down the street until I found a parking spot, and then I got out quickly and doubled back. The Ford was parked in front of a doughnut and coffee joint called The Green Door. The redhead was inside talking to the cashier. I watched him for a few moments, and then went back to the car. I kept looking in the side mirror until I saw the Ford pull into the stream of traffic again. I edged out a little. When the Ford passed me, I pulled in right behind my redhead.

He made a right turn at the corner, and then a left, and that took him to the traffic circle where the town began. He pulled up in front of the hotel. I pulled up two cars behind him. When he got out, I got out.

By the time I entered the lobby, he had already got his key and was in the elevator. I went straight to the desk.

"That red-headed fellow," I said.

"Yes?" the clerk answered, looking up.

"George Bradley, isn't he?"

"No," the clerk said, patiently correcting me. "That's Mr. Simms."

"Yes, of course," I said, snapping my fingers. "How stupid of me."

"John Simms," the clerk expanded, smiling.

"He's on the fourth floor, isn't he?" I asked. This was no remarkable deductive feat since Simms had been alone in the elevator, and the elevator floor indicator was now stopped at the numeral four.

"Yes, 407," the clerk said.

"Thank you."

I went to the elevator. I waited, watching the indicator. The door opened. "Four," I said.

"Two fours in a row," the elevator boy said, grinning. "Tough to make Little Joe twice in a row."

"Tougher to make seven twice in a row," I said.

"Depends on the talent," the elevator boy said. "You looking for action?"

"Not with dice."

"With broads?"

"You got some?"

"You name it."

"A big blonde."

"You got it."

"A big blonde named Stephanie," I said.

The elevator boy studied me for a moment. "You familiar with the area?" he asked.

"Not half as familiar as I'd like to be."

"Where'd you pick the name Stephanie?"

"Ran into her in a bar. Lost her later. Know where I can find her?"

"The Stephanie I'm thinking of ain't for sale."

"Maybe we're not thinking of the same girl," I said.

"I guess not, mister." He paused. "There are other big blondes."

"I'm choosy."

"So be," he said, and he shrugged and added, "Four."

He threw open the door, and I got out. I waited for the door to close, and then I looked for room 407. When I found it, I knocked.

"Who is it?"

"Phil Colby," I said.

"Who?"

"You don't know me. Open up, Simms."

"Just a minute."

The door opened. Simms had green eyes and a suntanned face. The eyes were narrowed now. "What do you want?"

"I want to talk to you."

"What about?"

"Lois," I said.

Simms studied me. "Come in," he said. I followed him into the room. It was furnished with a brass bed, a dresser, and an easy chair. A Gideon Bible was on the dresser. Alongside that was a bottle of cheap rye.

"You want a drink?"

"No, thanks."

"I'll have one," Simms said. He poured half a water glass full, and then drank half of that. He made a sighing, rasping sound and then said, "What do you know about Lois?"

"Only that she's missing."

"Where is she?"

"You tell me."

"What is this?" Simms asked.

"Was she at the station this morning?"

"Yes. Station guy says he saw her."

"How does he remember?"

"Three good-looking dames come in together, you'd remember, too."

"Three?"

"Blonde, redhead, brunette. Must have set the town on its ass. The cashier remembered them, too."

"What's Lois?"

"Huh? Oh. The brunette."

"Pretty?"

"I'm gonna marry her."

"Still. Is she pretty?"

"She's gorgeous."

"What was she doing at Mike Barter's place?"

Simms looked at me again. "How come you're so interested?"

"I lost something there, too."

"What'd you lose?"

"A girl."

"Is she a—" Simms stopped himself. "What was she doing there?"

"She was in a cabin. She vanished—clothes, luggage, everything."

"Yeah," Simms said, as if he were confirming the facts of his own situation. "It ain't like Lois. She woulda told me. She would of at least called. I know she would of called."

"What was *she* doing at Barter's place?" I asked.

Simms studied me. "She . . . had a job there."

"What kind of a job?"

"A job."

"That doesn't answer me."

"It's not supposed to," Simms said indignantly. "Listen, I'm gonna marry that girl."

"What's that got to do with her job?"

"A lot. Listen, I took enough baloney about Lois. I

don't happen to care what she done. I don't believe in that stuff.''

"What stuff?''

"About what a girl done or she didn't do. She loves me now, so what difference does it make? We're gonna get married. She'll make a good wife.''

"She probably will.''

"I *know* she will. She's the sweetest kid in the world. And she pleases me. I know, 'cause I been to bed with her.''

"I didn't ask.''

"I'm telling you, anyway,'' Simms paused. "I been to bed with her.'' He paused again. "Now you're supposed to say, 'You and a thousand other guys.' ''

"But I didn't say it,'' I said.

Simms seemed surprised. "No, you didn't,'' he said. He poured himself another drink. "You sure you don't want one?''

"Too early in the day for me.''

"I thought maybe you was one of these guys who don't touch it.''

"No,'' I said.

"Well, I thought maybe you was.'' He looked at me. "Cheers.'' And he threw off the hooker. "You want to know how I feel?'' he asked.

"About what?''

"Dames.''

"Sure.''

"I don't buy this stuff.''

"Which stuff?''

"What they done and what they didn't do. You know what's wrong with people?''

"No, what?''

"We all the time forget we're animals. We got minds, but we're also animals. So everything we do, we try to disguise we're animals. A guy meets a dame, something happens. In the songs, they say chemistry. It ain't chemistry. It's biology. Animals. Like when two dogs meet on the street, he don't ask her she wants a martini or she wants to see his etchings. They know what it's all about. They don't have love stories to read, and love movies to see. They don't get mixed up. The mutt knows, and the bitch knows, and they make it. Period.''

"What line of work are you in, Simms?"

"I drive a truck. For a beer company."

"I thought you might be a vet."

"I am. I was a Marine in World War II."

"I meant a veterinarian."

"That I ain't." Simms thought about it. "You mean because of the animals? I get a lot of time to think when I'm driving. You know what it is people hate to do most?"

"What?"

"You sure you don't want a drink?"

"I'm positive."

"I'll have another, if you don't mind. I tell you the truth, this thing has me kind of puzzled. A few drinks usually set me straight." He poured and drank. "What was I saying?"

"About what people hate to do most."

"Oh. Yeah. They hate to touch other people."

"They do?"

"They don't really. I mean, I think what they'd *like* to do *most* is touch other people. But they're afraid to. You know why?"

"Why?"

"Because then it gets animal. Instead, they reach out with their minds. Mister, you can only reach so far with your head."

"That's for sure."

"How do you tell another guy you're his friend?"

"I don't know. How?"

"You shake hands with him. You touch him."

"That has a medieval origin," I said. "Men shook hands so they'd know the other man wasn't carrying a dagger in his hand."

"Origin, shmorigin. They touch hands, and for a second they're saying we're animals. Then they pull the hand back. With a man and a woman, it's the same. Listen, don't you see this is all horse manure?"

"What is?"

"You can sit down with another guy's wife for three hours. You can talk all around what you really want to do, you can talk it inside out and backwards, upside down and right side up, so long as you got a drink in your hands, and so long as you keep smiling at each other. A big game. Everybody plays it. But put your hand on her knee, or put your arm around her shoulder, *bang!* Her husband comes in and starts yelling you're seducing his wife! For Christ's sake, you been seducing her for the past three hours, anyway! It don't make sense."

"Hardly anything does."

"But this especially. What I'm saying is this. There's like a big taboo, you understand? This taboo says, 'Don't touch!' It applies from when you're kids just dating, to when you're married, to when you got one foot in the grave. Marriage makes touching all right. When you're married, you get to be one person. You got no secrets, anyway. You belch, you yell, *'Hey, I got to get into that john!'* you spill things at the dinner table—in other words you share with another person the secret that you are only an animal with a mind. So the masterminds figured out where if you're belching, you might just as well be touching. But that's where the taboo is lifted, and no place else. And I say the taboo is a big crock."

"What are you *really* trying to say, Simms?"

"I'm trying to say I'm gonna marry a prostitute. A whore. A harlot. A hooker. A slut. Me. I'm gonna marry one. I love her, and screw you."

"I've got no objections."

"It wouldn't make a damn if you did. I wouldn't even care if you was one of the guys rolled with her, now what do you think of that?"

"I think it's an admirable attitude."

"There ain't nothin' admirable about it. It's common sense. She's been touched, and the others ain't. Who cares? Who knows these other guys? What the hell did she

give them but her body? You see what the trouble with
everybody is?''

"No. What?"

"They got it figured out so that the cheapest thing you
can give to another person is your *mind*. You sit around
and bullshit, and you're dishing out little chunks of your
mind. They got it figured so that the big premium is on
your body. This is the thing you don't give away without
a struggle to the death. Well, mister, they got it figured
out all bass-ackwards. I can be made, I admit it. But I'm
careful about who I give what's up here." He tapped his
temple. "Up here is what counts. The rest is all animals."

"You sound as if you're contradicting yourself," I said.

"Maybe I am. Who cares? You want a drink?"

"No. Tell me about Lois."

"A doll," Simms said. "Listen, I been around, and
this is a doll."

"What's she like?"

"A doll. Didn't you understand me? What's a doll—but
a doll?"

"Brunette?"

"Yeah. That means black hair, don't it?"

"Yes."

"Brunette," Simms said, nodding.

"Eyes?"

"Of course."

"The color, I meant."

"Oh. Brown. Like candy kisses."

"Short? Tall?"

"Bigger than me. Some guys this would disturb. Me, it
don't. I say it don't matter how tall a guy is, so long as
he feels big. I'm only five-eight. This is a shrimp nowa-
days. You meet guys are six-four. A generation of basket-
ball players. I know some short guys, everything about
them gets short. You can give me two guys, both five-six,
put them in the same room together. One guy looks like
a midget. The other guy, you never even stop to think how
tall or how short he is. You think a mutt ever stops and
wonders how tall another mutt is? You ever see a Chihua-

hua male pause before trying to mount a Great Dane bitch? Never happened, mister. Lois is tall, and I like her tall. When we go out together, she wears whatever kind of shoes she wants. Flats, heels, it makes no difference to me. She wears whatever makes her feel best, whatever makes her feel beautiful. And when she feels beautiful, I feel handsome. I feel big. I don't need no built-up shoes. All I need is her on my arm. And also, she fills up a bed. I like a bed that's all filled up. I don't like empty corners.''

"Why'd she go to Barter's place?"

"Why do you think?"

"But why there?"

"Why not? Good loot. I told you, we're getting married. We can use all the loot we can get our hands on.''

"Where's she from?"

"The next state. Me, too. Can't you tell? I got an accent a mile long. These hicks don't dig it.''

"And she was staying at Barter's place?"

"Only to work. She was registered here at the hotel. That's what I don't get. Everybody says she left town, but she didn't check out of this place!''

"When did she arrive?''

"Two days ago. She called me the first night, and then she said she'd call me again the next night. That was last night. When I didn't get her call, I tried to reach her at Barter's but the number ain't listed. The people here at the hotel said she wasn't in her room. This morning, I come right over the river. Man, I love that girl, you understand?''

"Did she tell you anything about the place when she spoke to you?''

"Only that she thought she could make a lot of money. She planned to stay a month, did I tell you? So how come she pulls up stakes now?'' Simms paused. "Something's mighty fishy. They told me at the station she got on a Davistown train. Why Davistown?'' He paused again. "How come you ask so many questions?''

"Force of habit," I said, smiling.

The room got very quiet. Simms poured himself another

drink. The whisky splashed into the glass. He didn't seem short at all. He seemed very tall. He sloshed the liquor around for a moment and then swallowed it. He looked at me steadily.

"You're a bull, ain't you?" he asked.

"Yes."

"Vice Squad?"

"No."

"What then?"

"Just an ordinary dick. I'm on vacation. My girl disappeared at Barter's place."

"So now you're messin' with it?"

"Yes."

"All this stuff I told you about Lois . . ." Simms hesitated.

"What stuff?"

"You know, about her being . . ."

"I didn't hear a thing," I said.

"I mean . . ."

"I didn't hear a thing. We've been discussing life, haven't we?"

Simms smiled. "What did you say your name was?"

"Phil Colby."

He extended his hand. "Simms. Johnny. You can call me Johnny."

I took his hand.

"I ain't shaking with you because I want to find out whether or not you got a dagger," Simms said. "I'm saying we're friends."

"I hear you."

"Are we?"

"I'm shaking hands," I said.

"Good." Simms paused. "I'm still gonna snoop around. If you need help, let me know. I got to find her, Colby."

"Phil," I said.

Simms smiled. "Phil, you just proved it, you know that?"

"Proved what?"

"That bulls are animals, too."

I left Simms and walked through the town. I had about an hour before meeting Mitchell, and it was the longest hour I ever spent in my life. After he arrived, we sort of went our separate ways because he thought he could accomplish more, not being known to Barter or the local cops. He told me later what happened, but that would probably be hearsay, and the best thing would be to have him here to tell it himself. But he's on a plant right now, and his job is law enforcement, and he's a more indispensable cop than I am. I have his deposition here, which I've been advised might be admitted as evidence. Whether it's admitted or not, I'd like permission to read it now because it fills in some of the gaps between my talk with Simms and what happened later on.

12

ANTHONY MITCHELL, BEING DULY SWORN, DEPOSES AND says as follows:

I arrived in the town of Sullivan's Corners at 5:45 P.M. on the evening of June 4th. I was driving an unmarked police sedan which Lieutenant DeMorra allowed me to check out. I have to admit that I was a little puzzled by the trouble Phil had got himself into, and a little surprised that the lieutenant was going out on a limb to help. Actually, I shouldn't have been surprised by anything the lieutenant did. He's about the greatest skipper there is, and I wouldn't trade him for Christmas every Sunday.

I found the only bank in town, and I also found the restaurant next door to it. For the record, the place was called "Fanny's." I took a table at the rear, and ordered a cup of coffee from a blond waitress who winked at me. I didn't wink back because I happen to be married, and I happen to feel that winks are for the teen-agers. I'm old-fashioned that way. I'm old-fashioned because my wife Sandy is old-fashioned, too. We agreed to the words, and the words were "and forsaking all others keep you alone unto him as long as you both shall live," and that made it legal, and I'm a big believer in things legal, otherwise I wouldn't be a cop.

I couldn't have been sitting for more than five minutes when Phil came in. He looked tired. I work with the guy, and I've seen him on tough assignments, and I've seen him on all-night plants, but he never looked quite as tired as when he walked into that place. He's a tall guy, with blond hair, and he was wearing gray slacks and a light-blue short-sleeved sports shirt. He looked very neat even though he hadn't shaved—blond guys don't have to shave except every other Thursday—but there was this tired slump to his shoulders, and this tired expression around his eyes. He spotted me immediately, and came straight to the table, extending his hand. I stood up and took it.

"Tony," he said.

"Sit down, Phil," I told him. "You look about ready to cave in."

"I'm kind of bushed," he said.

I signaled for the waitress and ordered another cup of coffee.

"I haven't had dinner yet," Phil said, and I don't know whether or not you are familiar with this boy's appetite, but to be kind I'll say it's somewhat wolfish. He asked for a menu, and I listened in awe while he ordered. "I've got to eat to think straight," he said. "Did the skipper tell you what happened?"

"He told me Ann's vanished. He also said you think she's safe. What else is there?"

"The place she vanished from is a whorehouse."

"Are you sure?"

"Positive."

"Mmmm," I said.

"What do you think?" Phil asked.

"I don't know. I just got here. How'd she vanish?"

"From her cabin. I don't know how. She was there asleep, and then suddenly she wasn't."

"Her clothes?"

"Gone. Luggage, too. Whoever cleaned out the cabin did a good job. Even got new tenants to take over after she was gone."

"Oh."

"Fellow named Joe Carlisle, and his alleged wife, girl named Stephanie. I checked later. Carlisle's not married."

"Who was the girl?"

"I don't know. I thought one of the hookers at first, but her clothes were in the closet, and there was a dresser full of underwear. The closet stuff wasn't a hooker's working gear."

"What stuff?"

"Some dresses, skirts, like that. From what I could gather talking to Simms—"

"Who?"

"Johnny Simms. Boyfriend of one of the girls who, incidentally, is also missing. Tony, this whole set up stinks. Did the lieutenant tell you about the blood?"

"Yes."

"Something, huh? Anyway, from what Simms said, I gather the girls live away from the motel. His girl was checked in at the local hotel. In town. Allegedly, she suddenly left the job at the motel. But she never checked out of the *hotel.*"

"Give me the setup," I said.

"About fifteen cabins at the motel. Run by a man named Mike Barter. He's married, never met his wife. The local law is wise to the setup, I'm sure. In any case, they've been in on the coverup. You might look up a j.p. named Oliver Handy. And watch out for a state trooper whose name is Fred. He's the son of a bitch who has my gun. And O'Hare's, too."

"Burry? How'd he get into this?"

"He had a .32 in the glove compartment of his car."

"Oh."

"Did you bring—"

"I brought you the one I usually keep at home. It's a Smith and Wesson. I gave it to Sandy, and I taught her how to use it. Now she's defenseless, you see?" I grinned. Phil grinned back.

"Where is it?"

"In the car. I'll give it to you when we get outside." I paused. "What else should I know?"

"Barter's got a handyman named Hezekiah. Carlisle apparently does work around the place, too, but Hez is the regular. He's a bruiser. Don't get into a bear hug with him."

"I won't. What's Ann wearing?"

"Her slip and brassiere, last time I saw her."

"Let's assume she's dressed now."

"I can only tell you what she was wearing when we left the city yesterday morning."

"Go ahead."

"A white cotton dress, one of these sun things with bare shoulders. She was carrying a straw bag, and she was wearing straw pumps. Lucite heels."

"Hat?"

"No. Never wears one."

"What about her luggage?"

"Just two plain brown leather bags."

"Anything else I should know?"

"A hooker named Blanche. Flaming redhead, kid of seventeen. If you see her, you can't miss her. She's got it blazed in neon across her chest. She was told to stall me last night when Ann disappeared. She also seems to know a hell of a lot more about all this than she's telling. She's the one who told me Ann is safe. Oh."

"What?"

"The j.p.—this Handy character—he also hinted that Ann would be all right if I just minded my own business."

"What are they trying to cover, Phil?"

"I don't know. I imagine the blood has something to do with it, though. Murder is something to cover."

"Who?"

"You've got me."

"Okay," I said. "I'll take a look. Where can I reach you?"

"I'll check in at the hotel. You can call me there. Where are you going now?"

"Out to the motel."

"All right, I'll wait for your call."

"It may not be until late tonight. I'd rather you didn't waste the time."

"What do you want me to do, Tony?" Phil asked.

"This hooker. The one who's missing, too."

"Lois is her name."

"All right. Find out all you can about her. There may be a tie-in with Ann."

"Okay, I'll talk to her boyfriend again."

"I'll try to ring you around midnight or so. If we run into each other anywhere in town, you don't know me. I only hope we're not being watched now."

"I don't think so, Tony."

"All right, come on. I'll give you that .38." I saw the look on Phil's face. "You can eat your dinner after I give you the gun."

We went out of the restaurant and over to the black sedan. Because we didn't want to attract attention, the transfer of the gun took place inside the car. Phil tucked it into his waistband.

"I feel better already," he said.

"Don't go using it unless you have to," I said.

"I haven't had to use it since I've been a cop," he answered.

"I have," I said. "I'll call you later." We shook hands, and he got out of the car, and I started driving towards Sullivan's Point. It was just getting dark when I got there. I parked the car behind a Cadillac with a tag reading SB-1412. I walked up to the motel office and knocked. There was no answer. I knocked again.

"Hello?" I called.

My voice echoed out over the lake. I sighed and was turning back toward the car when I saw the woman.

She came off the dock at the edge of the lake. She had a towel in her hands, and she was patting her face dry. The rest of her was wringing wet. She wore a two-piece swim suit of some stuff that looked like silver lamé. She was tall and slender, with the remarkable combination of good legs and a magnificent bust. She wore a bathing cap, and the cap was white and decorated with plastic daisies. She looked like a Follies girl making an entrance, except for the fact that she was unaware of any audience. I leaned against the fender of my car and watched her. She pulled off the cap, and blond hair tumbled free onto her shoulders. She shook her head, the way a big dog does when she's coming out of the water. I watched. She looked up then and saw me.

"Hello," I said. I grinned.

Her eyes were green, and the lashes were wet, and even if she hadn't just come from the water, they'd have been frigid. "Hello," she answered.

"How was the water?"

"Fine," she answered.

"It seems to have done you a lot of good."

"How would you know?" she asked. "You didn't see the 'Before' picture."

"No, but the 'After' is most convincing."

"Thanks. Are you finished?"

"I want a cabin," I said. "No one seems to be in the office."

"I'll take you up," she said.

"Do you know the owner?"

"I *am* the owner," she answered.

"Oh?"

"Stephanie Barter," she said with a small nod. "Come on." We walked up past the Caddy with the SB plate. It did not take a super sleuth to figure who owned the Caddy. There were several other things I wanted to ascertain though, and it would have been easier to discuss them with Mike Barter, rather than his wife.

We went into the office. Stephanie Barter kept dripping water onto the floor. She was a pretty thing to watch. I'd never seen her swim, but I was willing to bet she was good. She had a clean young body, a body she'd taken good care of. She was probably somewhere in her late thirties, but the body was much younger. The hair had an artificial look to it, but the bleach job was professional. Her nails were well manicured. Stephanie Barter, whatever else she did, spent a lot of time in the beauty salon.

"What exactly did you have in mind?" she asked.

"Is there a choice?" I said.

"Not really," she answered. "Did anyone recommend you? Or did you just happen by?"

"I was recommended," I said.

"By whom?"

I dug into my memory. "A fellow named Joe Carlisle. Know him?"

"Yes," Stephanie said. She was drying herself, but her green eyes never left my face. "Yes, I know him. He told you to stop here?"

"Yes."

"Um-huh. What's your name?"

"Tony," I said.

"Tony what?"

"Mitchell."

"How long do you know Joe?"

"Not a hell of a long time."

"I don't like profanity," Stephanie said.

"I'm sorry," I said, grinning.

"How long *exactly* do you know Joe?"

"I met him in a bar," I said.

"And?"

"I told him I was looking for a good place to"—I held the pause long enough to make it significant—"sleep."

"And he told you to come here, is that right?"

"He did."

"We might be able to accommodate you," Stephanie said.

"Might?"

"Yes. It depends on whether or not the facilities suit you. And, of course, the price."

"From what I've seen," I said, "the facilities are remarkable."

Stephanie did not smile. "The other cabins aren't quite like the office," she answered.

"Oh. I was hoping for something just like it."

"Well, I don't think you'll be too disappointed. You understand, of course, that it would be impossible to rent out the office, don't you?"

"Would it be impossible?" I asked.

Her eyes held mine. "Yes," she said. "I'm afraid it would be impossible."

"If you say so."

"I say so."

"Well then, it's impossible, I suppose."

It was a funny kind of conversation. She had told me a

lot of things in the past two minutes, but we'd talked with our eyes locked, the way a man and a woman very rarely speak. I'd just been sounding her because I wanted to find out exactly what her role was in the setup. But I got the feeling that she was seriously considering everything I said, and that she was even carrying on a small debate inside her head. Maybe I was wrong. In any case, the woman to get close to was Stephanie Barter. If anybody knew what was happening here, she was that person, I decided to press my luck.

"Naturally," I said, "rules are made to be broken."

Our eyes were still clenched somewhere in mid-air. "Yes," she said, "rules are made to be broken."

"And I do like the office. I really do."

"Your eyes are brown," she said quite suddenly.

"Yes."

"I like brown eyes."

"Thank you. About the rules . . ."

"If we rented the office, we'd be losing a revenue on one of the cabins," Stephanie said. "Besides, my husband would be furious if he learned about it."

"I wouldn't tell him," I said.

"Neither would I. Besides, after . . ." She stopped and shook her head. "But rules are rules."

"What's the revenue on the cabin?"

"Didn't Joe tell you?"

"No."

"A hundred and fifty."

"I must have blinked. Stephanie smiled for the first time and said, "Too high?"

"A little steep."

"But the cabins are very clean and very decorative. You'd be pleased."

"I'm sure. I would. But I want the office."

"My husband is away," she said suddenly. "On some business."

"What kind of business?"

"Something that had to be done."

"Will he be back soon?"

"I don't think so."

"Then why don't we talk this over a little more?"

"Talk over what?" she asked. She smiled again. "Your wanting to go to bed with me, do you mean?"

"Yes," I said.

"We can talk about it," she said. "Come inside while I change."

13

"INSIDE," WAS A SUITE OF ROOMS BEHIND THE MOTEL office.

There was a living room with a long cabinet and a longer couch and a rug that needed mowing. Stephanie went directly to the cabinet, opened one of the doors, and pulled out the record-player unit.

"I like music," she said. She picked up one of the LP albums from the cabinet top, and then pulled a Sinatra record from its protective cover. Sinatra began singing. Stephanie listened for a moment and then said, "He phrases beautifully." She nodded in agreement with herself, went to the other end of the cabinet, took a bottle and two glasses, and then said, "Come on."

I followed her into a luxurious bedroom. There were blue silk sheets on the double bed, and a white monogram where the sheets were folded over, the letters SBR. Stephanie Something Barter.

"What was your maiden name?" I asked.

"Roscanski. Horrible, isn't it?" She went to the closet, took something from a hanger there, and then went to another door. "I won't be long," she said. "Sit down."

She closed the door behind her. I sat on the chaise longue. I got up, walked to the bed, and touched the blue sheets. They were cool and smooth. I sat down again. In the bathroom, the water was running. It was getting dark outside. I went to the lamp on the night table and snapped it on. The water in the bathroom stopped. There was only Sinatra then, and the beginning night song of the katydids. The bathroom door opened. Stephanie Barter had pulled her blond hair back into a pony tail, tied it at the nape of her neck with a green ribbon that caught the color of her eyes. She wore a white robe with the SBR monogrammed on the left breast. She wore pink ruffled mules.

"Rye all right?" she asked.

"Rye will do very nicely," I said.

She walked to the dressing table where she'd left the bottle. She picked it up. The label read Canadian Club. She held out the bottle. "All right?" she asked.

"Fine," I said.

There was a keen glow of proprietorship in her eyes. She was proud of the Canadian Club, happy she could afford good whisky. She poured it liberally and handed me one of the glasses.

"Toast," she said.

"Here's to truth and beauty," I said. We clinked glasses.

"Why that?"

"Why not? They're the two most elusive things around."

"Beauty's cheap," Stephanie said. "You can buy beauty."

"You can't buy truth."

"Who would want to?" She thought a moment. "Besides, you can buy truth, too. You can buy anything you want in this world."

"Can I buy you?" I asked.

Stephanie laughed. "I've already been bought."

"Oh?"

"A long time ago. The man wanted beauty. He bought it."

"Which man?"

"Mike. My husband."

"What's he like?"

"He's a gorilla."

"That's nice."

"That is not so nice," Stephanie said, and she drank. She poured another drink for herself. I still had not tasted mine. "I like nice things," she said, "good things. The

best. Why drive a Ford when I can drive a Cadillac?'' She
savored the name of the car. She rolled it on her tongue.

"There's always a Lincoln Continental,'' I said.

"Is that better than a Cadillac?''

"Well, it costs more.''

She seemed troubled. "I didn't know that,'' she said.

"You'll have to look into it.''

"Yes.'' She sipped at her drink. "You've got a lot of
nerve, do you know?''

"Have I?''

"Yes. You're lucky, too.''

"How so?''

"If this were yesterday, you wouldn't be in this room.''

"What makes yesterday different from today?''

"Lots of things. The todays are always different from
the yesterdays, didn't you know?''

"I suspected.''

"What line of work are you in, Tony?''

"Why?''

"I'll bet I can guess.''

"Go ahead.''

"Advertising.''

"How'd you know?''

"I can tell. You dress like an advertising man.''

"I didn't know we were so obvious,'' I said. "How
does your husband dress?''

"How do gorillas dress? Like gorillas?'' She giggled.
"I believe in bargains, don't you?''

"Bargain basement bargains?''

"No, no, that's not what I meant. A bargain. A contract.''

"Yes, I believe in contracts.''

"So do I. At least, I did. You make a bargain, you stick
to it. You buy something, you sell something, that's it.
You put your name on the dotted line, and it's signed,
sealed, and delivered. F.O.B. San Diego.''

"Is that where you're from?''

"Yes. Do you know it?''

"No.''

"It's a crumby town. A sailor town. Not really as bad as Norfolk, but bad, anyway."

"What brought you east?"

"Bigger pickings. I learned my trade with sailors, but what can sailors do for you?" She paused and then said again, "I like nice things."

"And now you've got them."

"Now I've got them. Mrs. Michael Barter. I believe in bargains. I don't like contracts to be broken." She paused. "Do you really want to take me to bed?"

"I want to talk a while," I said.

"Mike doesn't talk much. Busy man. Very busy. You live with a man so many years, you never know about him. All of a sudden, I discover a lot about Mr. B."

"What'd you discover?"

"A lot. Have another drink."

"All right."

"Advertising men drink a lot, don't they?"

"Sometimes."

"Here." She poured. She touched her glass to mine. "To truth and beauty. I sold the beauty, but I was fair. That's truth. You make a contract, you stick to it. Both parties. I'm a pretty girl."

"You are."

"I was even prettier. When I married Mike, I was really pretty. When it starts to go, it goes fast. I swim every day, do you know? Winter and summer. Some days it's so cold I think I'll die. But I go down to the lake and take a dip. The only time I don't go is when the lake is frozen over. I skate then. Exercise. I got the good looks free, but that doesn't mean I shouldn't take care of them. You're not the first who liked the office better than the cabins."

"I didn't think I was."

"But you're the first who ever got past that door. Doesn't that make you feel good?"

"No."

"Why not?"

"You're just mad at your husband. I could have been anybody."

"That's not true. You drink to truth and beauty, but you're a liar."

"Aren't you mad at your husband?"

"Sure."

"Well?"

"That's got nothing to do with you."

"What contract did he break?"

"Who said he broke a contract?"

"You did."

"I said nothing of the sort."

"Somebody did, and it wasn't me."

"You think too much about contracts. That's all advertising men think of." She paused. "Are you important?"

"I run the company!"

"I run this company, too. Iron fist in a velvet glove. Do you want another drink?"

"No."

"Neither do I." There was a long silence. Frank Sinatra sang. "The whole world is contracts," Stephanie said. "Contracts signed, or about to be signed. Contracts kept, and contracts broken. I keep a contract. If you're going to be fair, you keep a contract. Otherwise, you're dirt."

"What contract did you make?"

"I contracted to be a wife."

"And have you been one?"

"I certainly have."

"Then there's no problem."

"No problem," Stephanie said. "You understand, I don't love Mike. Never did. I just made a contract. He bought me. He got beauty and a wife. I got anything I wanted—and a husband. That was the contract."

"What happened to it?"

"I don't like dirt," Stephanie said. "I had enough dirt when I was a kid. I didn't even have sheets on my bed, do you know? I slept with just a blanket over me. A blanket is coarse. I don't like coarseness, and I don't like dirt."

"For someone with such an aversion to dirt," I said dryly, "you're in a peculiar business."

"I run it clean. Everyone gets a fair shake. The girls are good. You make a contract with me, you don't get cheated."

"How'd you meet Mike?"

"Came out here one night on business. From the city. Mike ran it on a small scale. Don't misunderstand. He's rich. He looks like a gorilla, but he's rich. Owns half the lake. And now the business is a paying one, and I mean paying. There are fifteen cabins, and on good nights at least ten are full. We give the girls half the take. For some girls, we get as high as three hundred dollars. Multiply half of that by ten. It's a good business. You don't buy Cadillacs if you run a candy store."

"Are you happy?"

"Who is?"

"I am."

"Are you married?"

"Yes."

"If you're married, and you're so happy, what are you doing here?"

"Well . . ." I grinned.

"A temporary breach of contract," Stephanie said.

"I guess you could call it that."

"Maybe I don't like you so much after all."

"You never said you did."

"I do," she answered. "I haven't really talked to anyone in the longest time." The Sinatra record ended. Captured in the retaining grooves at the end of the record, the needle clicked and wove a crazy path. Stephanie stood near the bed, looking down at me. She went outside to the record player and lifted the arm. The room was very quiet when she came back.

"You're a gentleman, aren't you?" she said softly.

"Maybe."

"You must be. We've been alone for a half-hour and . . ." She stopped. Apparently she had heard something which eluded my ears. I listened. The sound came to me, too, then—the whine of a motor in the distance.

"Mike," she whispered, and she went to the door. I followed her into the office. She went behind the desk and opened a drawer, taking out a register. The motor sound was closer now, the sound of a heavy truck laboring into the court and then grinding to a halt.

There were footsteps on the gravel outside. The cabin door opened. The man standing there was short, and squat, and partially bald. He had small pig eyes and powerful arms. Behind him, like the trylon mate to the perisphere, was a tall hulking brute with a face as expressionless as a pan of dishwater.

"Who's this?" the short man said.

"Tony Mitchell," I said. "I'm a friend of Joe Carlisle."

"Yeah?"

"He's all right, Mike," Stephanie said wearily. "How'd everything go?"

Barter glanced at me quickly. "Fine," he said. He turned to the giant behind him. "Put the truck away, Hez," he said, and Hez turned and walked out of the cabin without a sound. Barter looked at me. "I don't think we'll be able to accommodate you tonight, Mr. Mitchell," he said.

"Why not?" Stephanie asked.

"We won't," Barter said simply.

"Joe specifically said I should come here," I said.

"Joe was wrong."

"He even told me who to ask for."

"I'm afraid he—"

"A girl named Lois," I said.

Barter stopped in mid-sentence. Stephanie looked up sharply. A quick glance passed between them.

"There's nobody by that name here," Barter said.

"Isn't there?"

"Never was."

"A tall brunette," I said.

"Oh," Stephanie said. "Lois."

"Yes."

"She left."

"That's too bad," I said.

"You remember Lois, don't you?" Stephanie asked Barter.

"Lois? Oh, yes, yes. She left."

"This morning," Stephanie said.

"Do you remember her now?" I asked Barter.

"Yes, I do. She's gone."

"Where'd she go?"

"Home."

"Where's that?"

"I don't know."

"Are you sure she's gone?"

"I put her on the train myself," Stephanie said.

"Train to where?"

"Davistown."

"Is that where she lives?"

"I don't know. That's where she went. I never asked her where she lived."

"Well, I'm a little disappointed," I said.

Stephanie caught my eye. "I am, too," she answered.

"Lois or no," Barter said, "we can't accommodate you."

"Then I guess I'll be shoving off."

"That would seem to be the thing to do," Barter said.

"Nice meeting you both."

"Try us again," Stephanie said.

"I will."

"If you see Joe," Barter said, "give him my regards."

"I will."

"He still lives in Murraysville, don't he?" Barter asked.

"Murraysville?"

"Yes," Barter said.

"I wouldn't know where he lives," I said. "I met him in a bar."

"Where?"

I took a wild shot in the dark. "Davistown," I said.

"Well," Barter said, sighing, "give him my regards."

When I got outside, the truck was gone. I pulled the car away from Stephanie Barter's Cadillac, and headed down the road.

I drove for four minutes before I doused the lights and pulled over into the bushes.

14

I'M A CITY BOY.

I was born and raised in the city, and that means a lot of things. It means you don't see grass or trees unless you go to a park. That sounds like a banality, but many banal things happen to be true nonetheless. It means the sky is always etched with concrete. It means that sometimes, on some streets, you feel you can't even see the sky. It means dirt, and garbage, and noise, and violence. A city is a lot of small towns clustered together. And so you get all the bad things of any small town, but you get the good things, too.

If you weren't raised in a city, you won't understand the good things.

You won't understand the joy of playing marbles alongside a curb after a summer rainstorm. You won't understand the deep pleasure of sticking your hand into a black puddle of water to span your marble and your competitor's. You won't savor the unparalleled thrill of riding a pusho which was made out of a two-by-four, an orange crate, and an old ball-bearing skate. You can hear the ball bearings rattle around in the wheels, because you purposely used a skate which had wheels with worn rims. You can feel the black asphalt skimming under the pusho, and you bounce on the two-by-four and skirt along with the other pushos, and in that moment you're Lawrence of Arabia on a white steed.

In the summer heat, you turn on the fire hydrant, and you bend a coffee tin and put it over the nozzle, and the water sprays up in a force-packed shower, and the kids dance under it, the black pavement slick and wet. When the cop comes, you run like hell, and you watch solemnly while he turns off the pump with a Stillson wrench until the water becomes only a trickle, and then only a memory.

In the summer, too, you sit on the front stoop with the other kids, and the city has its own song at night, especially on a summer night when the heat has baked into the street and the sidewalk and the brick walls of the tenements and a cool breeze blows in over the river. You can hear the city's song very clearly on a summer night. You can hear the horns, and the tugs, and the voices, and the people. You can hear the sound around you like the sound of mingled voices at a public beach, hovering on the air, indistinct, unintelligible, and beneath that the whisper of your friends beside you on the stoop, and the cool comfort of a cup of ices clenched in your fist, and the vast exchange of sex and religion and philosophy.

In the fall, the city doesn't have turning leaves. In the fall, the city has a bite on the air, a bite as sharp as a dragon's tooth. You put the summer to rest, and you buckle down, and if you're a kid you shop the five-and-dime for your new looseleaf folder, and your new pencils, and you can smell school in the air, and the smell is a good one. The tempo is picked up. You can't feel tempo anywhere but in the city. In the city the footsteps are magnified by a million, and you can feel the quicker beat, and there's suddenly purpose to the city—the summer is gone, the loafing is over, the city is tightening its belt for the cold winter ahead. You see health glowing on the faces. You see apple-red cheeks, and you can remember roasting potatoes in empty lots when there were still empty lots, and you can remember Election Day bonfires leaping high in the middle of the street, leaping to the second story of an apartment building, you can remember hauling wood for the fire, dancing around it like the goblin you were on Halloween. You wore knickers then. You wore a watch cap, banded with multicolored stripes of wool. Sometimes you wore your leather aviator's helmet, fleece-lined, with

the goggles down only when you were sitting around a
fire.

The winters were cold, and you didn't ice skate in the
city. Ice-skating was something you learned later, when
you were older, something you would never be really good
at because you learned so late. But the snowplows rushed
through the streets like giant tanks, pushing the snow to
the curb, making tall fortresses. You climbed the fortresses, and the city became a mountainland of cold and
ice and you felt for a moment a part of the people all
around you, and you longed for the greater intimacy of a
really snowbound community.

In the spring, you had Saint Paddy's day. You weren't
Irish, but your blood sang on that day, anyway, and you
made sure you had a green tie, and there was an Irish girl
in your class you kissed, and you sang "Did Your Mother
Come from Ireland?" and you cut classes to watch the
parade downtown. You saw cops then. Lines and lines of
cops. Marching in precision, lines of blue. You became a
cop later for different reasons, but you'd never forget the
marching blue uniforms, or the sudden mild breeze, mild
for March, the sudden warm sun, so warm for March, that
heralded the day of the Irish and the beginning of spring.

You loved the city because the city had been part of you
since the day you looked up from your carriage and saw
the buildings reaching for the sky. You could go to the
country for picnics, but the city always called you back,
and you heard her keening song in the strangest places—
on gangway watch in the yards at Boston, on the fantail
of a destroyer on a quiet moonlit night with the Pacific as
still as a sleeping babe, behind the heaving smoking barrels of a 40 mm. gun trained on a Jap Zero, the *pom-pom,
pom-pom* bursting your eardrums, the acrid stench of
cordite powerful in your nostrils. You didn't forget the
song of the city. You couldn't forget it because you helped
write it.

I'm a city boy.

The country doesn't gas me.

I don't like lonely roads without lights, and I don't like

the hum of insects, the incessant goddamn chirruping and croaking and *cccsssking,* and *chipock-chipocking.* I don't like getting out of a car and being hit in the face with the eerie strand of a spider's web. I don't like stepping in soft mud, and I don't like the feeling that the next time I put down my foot it might be on a wasp's nest, or in a bed of quicksand, or on a snake.

I'm chicken that way.

I'm a coward.

I got out of the police sedan on the night of June 4th, and there was nothing I'd rather have done less. I brushed the spider's web from my face, feeling crawly, wondering if the spider were entangled in my hair, and then I started through the woods. I was about as absolutely quiet as Davy Crockett with his leg in a plaster cast. A deaf Parisian sitting in the shade of the Eiffel Tower could have heard me. A *dead* Indian buried in the Taj Mahal would have perked up his ears at my coming. Martians paddling down their canals undoubtedly wondered what all the racket was about.

There was only one thing I wanted.

Mike Barter had driven somewhere with Hezekiah on business. I didn't know what the business had been, but they'd driven in the truck. I wanted a look at that truck.

There were sounds in the woods. I didn't like the sounds. They scared me. That's the absolute truth. I pulled my .38 from its holster in my back pocket. I threw off the safety, and I edged my way through the woods listening to the sounds. Branches snapped. Animals seemed to lurk behind every tree. Birds screeched every now and then. The insects buzzed and hummed. There wasn't a light showing anywhere. A country boy would have made a beeline for the motel. I'm a city boy. I didn't know where the hell I was going. I hoped I was going in a straight line. I hoped I was heading for the motel. I hoped I could find my way back to the car if it turned out I wasn't heading for the motel.

Hope is a poor substitute for woodsmanship. I should

have been a Boy Scout. I should have been a pioneer. I should have stayed in bed.

I don't believe in stacking the deck. It gets comical after a while. It gets like a soap opera.

"When we left Nellie May yesterday, her mother was dying of frostbite and the phone was out of order. Nellie couldn't send her brother Tom to the village for the doctor because Tom had a broken leg. The lion who'd escaped from the circus was clawing at the kitchen screen door, and the oil burner had just exploded setting the basement on fire. As we all know, Nellie is a drug addict, and her last fix had been three days ago . . ."

So I don't believe in stacking the deck. I figured Phil was in enough trouble as it was. I figured DeMorra was sticking his neck out by sending me to help. I figured Ann might be in serious danger, and I figured I was a horse's ass for traipsing through the woods without a compass.

I needed what happened next. I needed it like Nellie May needed the circus lion at her kitchen door.

I felt myself falling.

The fall came suddenly, the ground abruptly sloping off so that I lost my footing. I stumbled forward, groping for support where there was none. Something cold touched my ankle, and panic roared up into my brain until I realized the something cold was water. I was too far gone by that time. I fell flat on my face, covered with slime, covered with water that surely had come out of an ice-cube tray. I'd clung tightly to the .38, but it was submerged with me, and it probably wouldn't fire for the next ten years. I sat up. The water was up to my waist. I wanted to laugh. Until I heard—or rather sensed—movement in the water.

I thought it was a trick of my eyes at first, a gag my ears were playing.

I'd heard about snakes swimming, but I'd never seen one before.

I couldn't even see this one too clearly, except that he was about three feet away from me in the water and coming on an apparent collision course. If you're going to be shocked, go ahead. I didn't ask for the snake. I didn't even ask for a caterpillar. I'm no different from you, unless you're a snake trainer. I don't like them. I pulled the .38 up, and I fired. The gun misfired, and I squeezed the trigger again, and again there was nothing, and then the snake hit.

I screamed.

I don't give a damn what you think about men screaming. I screamed. I screamed as loud as I know how to scream, and then I felt a needle-like pain in my leg, and I screamed again, and I lashed out at the snake with the butt of the .38, and I kept lashing, striking up the water, hitting at the snake, and yelling and screaming and cursing all the while. He left.

As suddenly as he'd come, he was gone.

I couldn't move.

I sat with the black waters swirling around my waist. I was trembling, and I suppose my eyes were shut tight, and then the shocking idea came that there might be more snakes in the water, and I leaped to my feet and clawed my way up the bank of the pond, and I fell flat on my face again, but this time I got up and shoved my way through the bushes, feeling the bushes clawing at me like live things, hearing the insects, and hearing the animal noises, but pushing through, and then becoming aware of the awful pain in my leg, and suddenly cognizant of the fact that the snake may have been a poisonous one.

It occurred to me that the most idiotic thing I could do at the moment would be to get lost in the woods and die of snake bite. I could not, right then, think of a more moronic way of dying. I didn't have a pocket knife, and even if I did, I wouldn't have known the first thing about lancing a snake bite and drawing off the poison. I didn't know where I was, and I didn't know how to find out where I was, and I longed for the feel of asphalt under my feet, longed for the screech of the elevated trains, longed for the blare of a traffic signal.

I came close to panic again.

It's very easy to panic. Panic is the easiest thing in the

world to do. You don't panic when you're up against a situation you know you can control. You can face another man with a revolver, and he can be firing at you, and you won't panic because you've faced men with revolvers before. You can face a broken bottle being thrust at your jugular vein and you won't panic because this is old hat. But it's easy to panic when you don't know the score. You can feel the panic bubbling inside your stomach, and it's so easy to let it go, so easy to let it erupt into your mind and your body, so easy to let it propel your legs, let it control the wild flailing of your arms, let it put fright in your eyes and fear in your heart.

I didn't.

I wouldn't.

I kept shoving my way through the woods, dragging my leg behind me, dragging my backside, dragging every ounce of will power I could muster. I kept on what I hoped was a line paralleling the road. And finally I saw a light.

I still had the .38 in my fist. I clung to it, as if it were a howitzer instead of a gun which wouldn't fire.

I came out of the woods behind the motel, and I staggered down to the gravel court, and I shouted, "Help!"

I wasn't thinking of detective work at the moment. I was thinking I'd been bitten by a poisonous snake, and I needed a doctor. The office door opened. Barter and Hezekiah stepped into the light.

"Help!" I said again, and I limped toward them. Hezekiah came out of the doorway. Something big and ugly was in his hands.

"I've been bitten by a snake," I said, and Hezekiah, son of a bitch that he was, hit me on the head.

15

I FELT LIKE A PRIVATE EYE.

Only private eyes get hit on the head. They feel "black-ness closing in," or "consciousness going down the drain." Or they feel "the lights going out." Private eyes are always getting hit on the head. It's a wonder their skulls don't look like sieves.

I don't know if you've ever been hit on the head with a wrench. Hezekiah hit me with a wrench. In books, in the movies, you get hit on the head with a wrench and you go unconscious and when you wake up you feel a little dizzy. Otherwise, you're fine. You just missed a little bit of the action, but everybody is in a big hurry to fill you in.

I would like to correct this false impression.

The skull, even if it is a hard one like mine, is a pretty vulnerable thing. If you get hit with a wrench, or a bottle, or a hammer, or a chair, or a club, or a shoe, or whatever, you don't just drift off into a peaceful sleep. Bang your head sometime by accident and see how quickly the bump rises. Then add the force of a man's arm and shoulder to the blow, add the terrible impact of a piece of forged steel.

Your head cracks.

The hair cushions the blow only slightly, and then the steel splits the skin and opens your skull, and if you're lucky you don't suffer a brain concussion. If you're lucky, you bleed. Your head aches, and you bleed. You bleed down the side of your face, and down the side of your neck, and under your shirt collar. There is a hole in your head, and your blood runs out of it, and when you finally come to, the blood is caked and dried on your temple and your cheek and your neck.

You squint up at the light, and you feel only a terrible pain somewhere at the top of your head. You can't even localize the pain, because your whole head seems to be in a vise, your whole head is pounding and throbbing. This is the hangover supreme. This is the prince of all hangovers, and you don't laugh it off and drink a glass of tomato juice. There's nothing to laugh about. You've been hit on the head, and the chair didn't shatter the way it does in the movies—but your head did.

The light was a naked bulb suspended from a long thin wire. It hung motionless in the center of the room, a feeble sun that assailed my eyes when I opened them. I blinked. My head ached, and my leg throbbed, and I remembered the snake bite, and I could feel crusted dried blood on my face and on my trouser leg. I was sitting in a chair. I tried to get out of the chair, but my hands were tied behind it, and my legs were tied to the chair legs.

A girl was sitting opposite me.

The girl was a pretty brunette. Her eyes were wide with concern.

"Thank God," she whispered.

I blinked at her.

"I thought you were dead," she said.

I blinked again. The girl was tied, too. She wore a white cotton dress and straw pumps with lucite heels. She was very pretty, a big girl, a big girl tied in a small chair, the light hanging motionless over her head.

"Are you all right?" she asked.

I tried to talk but nothing came to my mouth. I cleared my throat. "I'm all right," I said.

"I'm Ann," the girl said.

It sounded like a vaudeville routine. "Are you all right?" *"Yes, I'm fine."* "How do you do; I'm Katz."

"How do you do; I'm Katz," I said.

The girl looked puzzled. "Aren't . . . aren't you Tony Mitchell?"

"Yes," I said. "I got bit by a snake."

"It wasn't poisonous," the girl said. "They were talking about it. One of them said it was better this way, and then another said there weren't any poisonous snakes in the area."

"My head hurts," I said.

"You look awful."

"Thank you."

"Is Phil all right?"

"Phil?"

"Yes. Don't you . . . ?"

"Phil," I said. "Jesus, are you Ann?"

"Yes, I told you . . ."

"Forgive me."

"It's all right. I was afraid you were dead. You were bleeding so badly when they carried you in."

"*Who* carried me in?"

"A short fat man, and a tall—"

"Barter and Hezekiah," I grinned. "It sounds like a law firm."

"*Is* Phil all right?"

"He's fine. I'm Katz. Forgive me, I'm dizzy. My head hurts. I'm supposed to call him. He's worried about you."

"I'm fine," Ann said.

"Not again, please."

"Not *what* again?"

"Nothing. Where are we?"

"In Davistown."

"Where in Davistown?"

"Somebody's apartment. A man they call Joe."

"Joe Carlisle?"

"I don't know. They didn't say his last name."

"How'd you get here?"

"By train. And by taxi."

"When?"

"This morning."

"What time is it now, anyway?"

"It's almost midnight."

"I'm supposed to call Phil." I paused. "They brought you here this morning, huh?"

"Yes. When my dress dried."

"When your what?"

"My dress."

"That's what I thought you said." I blinked. "Maybe you better start with when they took you out of the cabin."

"I was fast asleep," Ann said. "They came in, two of them, the short one and . . . Barter, is that his name?"

"Yes."

"Barter and the blonde. Stephanie."

"Go ahead."

"They took me out of bed, and then a truck came out of the woods. The tall one, Hezekiah, was driving it. They put me into the back of the truck. That's how I got the blood on my dress. Somewhere in the truck."

"Where'd they take you?"

"To Hezekiah's place. He lives on a road somewhere near the motel. It wasn't a very long trip."

"Then what?"

"They made a phone call. Stephanie made it. To this man, Joe. They told him to get over to Hez's place right away. When she got off the phone, Barter said, 'Good. When he gets here, you go back to the motel, get some clothes and some luggage, and get into that cabin.' I guess he meant the cabin they'd taken me from."

"Yes, yes."

"Joe arrived about a half-hour later, and he and Stephanie drove off in the Cadillac. They had me tied in the bedroom. Barter and Hezekiah left, too, but Hez had trouble starting his car. It's a very old car."

"They left the truck at Hez's place?"

"Yes."

"Did you see anything else in the truck?"

"No. Was there anything else?"

"I don't know. Go ahead, what happened next?"

"They came for me early the next morning. Stephanie saw the blood on my dress, and she washed it out. We waited until it dried before we left."

"Where'd you go?"

"To Sullivan's Corners. Stephanie drove us in the Cadillac."

"Us?"

"The redhead and me. Blanche. She looked like a slut."

"She was."

"She had on the most horrible purple dress. Stephanie was dressed garishly, too. A bright red dress. We made quite an interesting trio."

"I'll bet you did. What happened then?"

"We stopped for coffee in town. Blanche had a gun. She was carrying a white stole over her arm, covering the gun. They said they'd shoot me if I spoke to anyone."

"So you kept quiet?"

"I kept quiet. Was that wrong?"

"That was very right. Then what?"

"Then we went to the train station. We walked right down the main street. I guess we attracted quite a bit of attention. Stephanie bought two tickets to Davistown. The redhead and I got on the train when it pulled in. She still had the gun in her hand, under the stole."

"What time was this?"

"About nine-thirty or so."

"Go ahead."

"When we got to Davistown, we took a cab here. This man Joe tied me up. Blanche said she was going back to Sullivan's Corners."

"Have you got any idea why you're here?"

"No," Ann said. "But they haven't harmed me in any way. I mean, except for Joe's hands . . ." Ann paused. "He's got hands," she said.

"It's the company he keeps," I told her. "Did you happen to run into a girl named Lois?"

"No."

"I didn't think so." I paused, thinking. "How'd you know who I was?"

"There was a phone call earlier tonight. Joe took it. I heard him say 'Who?' and then he said, 'Tony Mitchell? No, I don't know any Tony Mitchell.' When they brought you in . . . well, Phil's described you so many times."

"I see. That phone call accounts for the knock on the head. They knew who I was the second time around."

"What's going on, Tony? Do you know?"

"I've got an idea," I said. "I just hope that Phil gets the same idea."

"Do you think—?"

The door opened. Stephanie Barter and her husband came into the room. A tall thin man was behind them. He had blue eyes and brown hair, and he was grinning.

"How's your head, Detective Mitchell?" Stephanie asked.

"Still on my shoulders, thanks," I said.

"Hez should have hit you harder," Barter said. "We didn't know you were a cop when he hit you. We didn't find that out until we went through your wallet."

"And now that you know?"

"It depends on how much *you* know, Mitchell."

"I don't know anything. I came here to help a friend find his girl. I've found her."

"You also found a lot of trouble."

"None that I can see. Let us go, and then you can go back to your damn whorehouse."

"I don't like profanity," Stephanie said.

"The hell with that. I don't like getting hit on the head by—"

"Watch the way you talk," the tall thin man said.

"You're Joe, I take it."

"I'm Joe," he said.

"Your trip last night can cause you a lot of accessory-after trouble, Joe."

"Accessory after *what?*" Stephanie asked.

I smiled. "The fact, naturally."

"What fact?"

"I have no idea," I said.

"I'll bet you don't," Barter answered. "It doesn't make any difference anyhow. You're in this too deep already."

"In what?"

Barter turned to Stephanie. "In a damn stupid setup that was none of my—"

"Shut your foul mouth," Stephanie snapped. "You're as much to blame—"

"If you hadn't—"

"Shut up!"

Barter clamped his mouth shut. He was either afraid of Stephanie, or afraid he was about to say too much in my presence.

"All right," he said at last. "They're your guests. What do we do with them?"

"We wait for the other two," Stephanie said.

"And then what?"

"You know what."

"That's what I don't like about this," Barter said. "All because—"

"Shut up!"

"I won't shut up. Goddamnit, why should . . . ?"

Stephanie slapped him suddenly and fiercely. "You're filthy," she said. "You're filthy and slimy." She came closer to him, and Barter shrank away as if he were expecting another blow. "Get out of here. Get out of this room. I haven't forgotten, you slimy . . ."

"Take it easy, Steph," Carlisle said.

"Get him out of here," she answered. Her voice was a deadly cold whisper. Carlisle took Barter's elbow and led him to the door. At the door, Barter turned as if he wanted to say something. Then he shook his head and went out, Carlisle after him.

"You shouldn't have played games with me, Mitchell," Stephanie said.

"How do you know I was playing?"

"And don't play with me now!" she snapped. There was anger in her eyes, and impatience. Together, they were a fearful combination. The lady had something eating her, and she wouldn't be happy until the last bite was swallowed.

"When does the party begin?" I asked.

"As far as you're concerned," she said, "the party's over."

"Who are the other two we're waiting for?"

"You guess."

"Offhand, I'd say Phil Colby and a fellow named Simms."

"That's right," Stephanie said somewhat proudly. I didn't know whether she was proud of my deductive ability or of her own scheming.

"And when they get here?"

"You tell it. You tell stories beautifully."

"You kill us," I said simply.

"Yes," she said.

"Why?"

Stephanie didn't answer. She kept watching me with a small smile on her mouth.

"You're going to a lot of trouble for a simple thing like abduction, aren't you?"

"There's a little more than abduction involved," Stephanie said. "Just a little more than that."

"Like what?"

"Like a half-million dollar business I don't feel like seeing washed away."

"Who's going to wash it away?"

"Any number of people," she said. "But especially you four."

"What could we do?"

"There's a district attorney in this state," Stephanie said. "A smart cop would know where to find him."

"A smarter cop could know when the quiet payoff is due. A cop like that might want to trade his life for silence."

She looked at me steadily. "Only one thing wrong there," she said.

"What's that?"

"You're not that kind of a cop."

"Try me," I said.

"And wind up with another broken contract? Sorry."

"You'd rather do murder, huh?"

Stephanie didn't answer.

"You'd be wasting your time, anyway," I said. "The lieutenant at my precinct knows the whole story." Actually, he *didn't* know the whole story, but Stephanie didn't know that, and I was grabbing for straws.

"Let him come after you," Stephanie said.

"He's a stubborn guy. He's just liable to do it."

"Let him. He'll find an automobile accident."

"A what?"

"A car that skidded into the lake or over the gorge. A car with four occupants. You, the girl, Colby, and Simms."

Ann drew in a sharp breath.

"It'd never work," I told Stephanie.

"I'll chance it. You don't throw away something you've worked for all your life, Mitchell. You hold onto it."

"There's just one thing I'd like to hold onto," I said.

"What?"

"My life."

Stephanie smiled. "You can be cute. It's a shame."

"It's a damn shame," I agreed.

"If you're going to start swearing," Stephanie began, and I said, "Oh, shit!"

The smile dropped from her mouth.

"They're looking for the other two now," she said tightly. "It shouldn't be too difficult to find them."

"It might be a little more difficult than it was with me."

"Why?"

"Those two haven't been bitten by snakes."

16

THAT'S THE END OF TONY'S DEPOSITION EXCEPT FOR THE
"Sworn to before me on this seventeenth day of July"
business at the end, which I won't read.

I have to admit that when his call didn't come at midnight, I began to get a little worried. I'd talked to Simms
in his room as soon as I'd finished dinner and checked in.
Simms told me that Lois and a redhead had boarded the
9:44 A.M. train to Davistown. From the way the stationmaster had described the redhead to him, and from the
way Simms in turn described her to me, she couldn't have
been anyone but Blanche.

I'd seen Blanche in town at about two in the afternoon
at the restaurant. If she'd gone to Davistown that morning,
she had hightailed it back in a hurry. And apparently *without* Lois. Simms was all for scouring the town until we
turned up Blanche. I asked him to wait until the call from
Mitchell came, and he agreed that would be the best course
to follow.

I left him in his room at 11:30. I gave him my room
number in case anything important came up, and I told
him I'd go back upstairs to him as soon as I heard from
Tony. Then I went down to wait. Midnight came too fast.
Tony is a punctual guy, and when that phone didn't ring
at midnight, I began to have my first doubts. At 12:15, the
phone still hadn't rung.

Someone knocked on the door instead.

"Who is it?" I called.

"Bellboy, sir," the voice answered, and I fell for the
oldest gag in the universe and opened the door.

Tex Planett was standing in the corridor. Two deputies I'd never seen were standing behind him. The last time Planett and I had met, he was wearing his .45 in a side holster. This time, he was wearing it in his fist.

"Get your coat, Colby," he said. He was smiling. He was enjoying himself.

"What for?" I said.

"Want to talk to you in my office."

"What for?"

Planett shrugged. "Suspicion of burglary. How's that? Get your coat."

I moved toward my jacket on the bed. Sandy's revolver was in the inside pocket of that jacket.

"Hold it, Colby," Planett said. He gestured to one of the deputies, and the deputy went to the jacket, frisked it for about half a second, and found the gun. He handed the gun to Planett, and the jacket to me.

'Now put it on," Planett said.

I shrugged into the jacket.

"Where's your pal?" he asked.

For a moment, I thought he meant Mitchell, and my hopes rose slightly. "What pal?" I said.

"Simms. We were just up to his room. He's not there."

"I don't know where he is."

Planett smiled. "We'll find him. One of us is sure to find him. Come on."

We went down to the waiting police car. The town seal was painted on the side of the car. The car was blue with an orange top. It was, at that hour, the loudest thing in Sullivan's Corners. We drove to Planett's office. When we got there, he didn't bother booking me. He took me straight to the cell block, opened one of the cells, and then locked it behind me.

He was starting off when I called him back.

"What's the story, Planett?"

"The story? No story, Colby."

"Why am I here?"

"You're waiting for somebody. As soon as I make a phone call, somebody'll pick you up."

"Who?"

Planett smiled.

"And when I'm picked up, where do I go?"

Planett smiled again.

"Come on, what's the story?"

"The story is simple. We don't want D.A. trouble. We don't want State's Attorney trouble, either. We like the setup the way it is. Sometimes things happen that can foul up a situation. We take care of those things. Simple?"

"Simple. What happens to me?"

"I think you die, Colby," he said flatly.

"Just like that?"

"Just like that." Planett smiled. "It's nothing personal, believe me. A setup has to be protected. I earn about $6,000 a year. That's not so much. A man needs a setup."

"I earn $5,230 a year," I said, "and I don't have any setup."

Planett shrugged. "You're the one's going to die—not me."

"All this to cover a whorehouse?" I asked.

"All this to cover a murder," Planett said, and he wasn't smiling any more. He turned and started off down the corridor. He unlocked the door at the end, and I watched him, and then he began backing into the corridor again, and he puzzled me for a moment until I saw what he was backing away from.

Johnny Simms was coming through the door. Johnny Simms had a fire ax in his hands. Planett was reaching for the .45 at his hip when Simms swung. He swung as if he were about to fell a tree, except that he used the broad flat side of the ax. His aim was true. He caught Planett on the side of his head, and Planett slammed sidewards into the corridor wall, and then collapsed like a dish rag. Simms stooped and pulled the ring of keys from Planett's belt. He unlocked the cell door, and I said, "You might have killed him."

"Maybe I did," Simms answered. He grinned. "You should see his two deputies out there. I caught them in the middle of a card game."

"Where'd you get the ax?"

"In the hotel corridor, alongside a fire hose. I was coming down to your room when I saw Planett and his boys. I didn't think he was taking you here for a piano recital."

"Where'd you learn to use that ax that way?"

"I was a Marine," Simms said. "Remember?"

"I remember." I stooped down and pulled Sandy's gun from Planett's belt. Then I yanked the .45 from his holster and handed it to Simms. "This should feel familiar to a Marine."

He took the gun. "It does."

"Come on."

We passed through the outer office. The deputies had been playing poker. One of them had obviously been trying to fill an inside straight. He had filled a knock on the head instead.

"My car's down the street outside the hotel," I said. "Let's get it."

"Where we going?" Simms wanted to know.

"To the motel."

"Good."

We were walking rapidly, our heels clicking on the sidewalk of the silent town. I turned to Simms. "There may be trouble."

"I'm just itching for trouble," he said. "Can't you tell?"

"I mean big trouble."

"Lois is gone," Simms said simply. "That's the biggest trouble I can imagine."

"All right," I said. "Come on."

When we reached O'Hare's convertible I started the engine and then reached for a knob on the dash. "You may get chilly, but I'm putting the top down," I said. "I want to be able to get in and out of this thing in a hurry."

"All right," Simms said. He watched the top as it folded back over his head. Then he looked up at the sky. "It looks like rain."

"Yes," I said as I pulled away from the curb.

We didn't talk much on the way to the motel. When we

got there, the grounds were pitch black. I kept the headlights up, splashing across the office door. "There's a flash
in the glove compartment," I said to Simms. "You'd better get it."

I drew the .38 and went to the door. I banged on the
door with the gun butt. There was no answer. Simms was
out of the car, splashing light on the ground with the flash.

"Tire tracks here," he said. "Leading into the woods."

I walked over to where the flash made a circle of light
on the soft earth just off the gravel court.

"Truck tires," I said.

"Want to check it?"

"Yes."

Simms walked ahead of me, the flash in his left hand,
the .45 in his right. The truck had made big ruts in the
soft earth. It wasn't a difficult trail to follow.

"There she is," Simms said.

The truck sat in a clearing ringed with tall pines. The
air smelled good. There was no moon and no stars, and
the sky was sown with rain clouds, but the pines smelled
antiseptic and the silence was pure. The truck sat like a
brooding prehistoric monster. Simms splashed the light
onto the tailgate.

"Let's see what's inside," I said. We were talking in
whispers. There's something about the darkness of night
and the silence of woods that makes men automatically
lower their voices. Together, we lowered the tailgate. I
climbed up into the truck.

"Want to hand me the light, Johnny?"

He passed the flash to me. I ran it over the floorboards.
In one corner of the truck was a burlap sack. It was empty,
but it was soggy and limp, wadded into the corner, hud-
dled there like a frightened amoeba.

The sack was red with blood.

I got sick inside.

I stood there for several moments, and I couldn't say
anything or think anything. I finally knelt and touched the
sack. The blood was cold. I got up and played the flash

over the rest of the truck. Something metallic flashed in the beam of light. I stooped again.

It was a shovel with a broken handle.

There was fresh earth on the blade. There was dried blood on the splintered wooden shaft. I went to the back of the truck, doused the light, and jumped to the ground. I handed the dead flash to Simms.

"Better leave it out," I said.

"Why?" He studied me in the darkness. "What'd you find?"

"Blood."

"What?"

"And a shovel that was recently used. Somebody's dead, Johnny, and somebody was buried."

"Who?" he asked.

"I don't know."

"Buried . . . where?"

"I don't know."

"Here?"

"I doubt it. Probably some place away from here."

"It couldn't be Lois," he said. "She went to Davistown. She . . ."

"No," I said. "It couldn't be Lois."

"Then—" He cut himself off. He stuck the flashlight into his back pocket. We walked up the road in silence. The voice came as a complete surprise.

"Don't use them guns," it said.

I stopped dead, automatically bringing up the .38.

"I said don't! My finger's on the trigger. All I got to do is tighten it."

He stood in the middle of the road, a giant in a red plaid shirt and earth-stained dungarees. Hezekiah. He held a shotgun in his hands. As he'd said, one finger was making love to the trigger.

"Drop it, Colby," he said. "You, too, Simms."

I dropped the .38. I heard Simms' .45 thud to the ground beside me.

"Kick them over here."

I kicked my gun toward him, and then the .45. Hezekiah stooped to pick them up. He put the .38 in one trouser pocket and the .45 in the other.

"Get together," he said. "Both of you. I want to see you both."

Simms stepped closer to me. His hands were on his hips, the thumbs cradling his hip bones, the fingers spreading around behind his back.

"You found the truck, huh?" Hezekiah said.

"Yes."

"You find what was in it?"

"What'd you have in mind, Hez?"

"The sack we carried her in. The shovel we used to dig her grave." I couldn't see his face, but it sounded as if he were grinning.

"We found them," I said.

"They told me to get you. I figured you'd come back here to look for your detective friend. I figured right, huh?"

The news that they'd tipped to Mitchell wasn't exactly heartening. "You figured right," I said disconsolately.

"Sure," he agreed. "I'm no dope."

"Are you smart enough not to get mixed up in murder?"

"I'm mixed up in it already," Hez said.

"You can still get out."

"Can I? With the girl dead and buried?"

"But *you* didn't kill her, Hez."

"I know I didn't."

"So why be a sucker?"

I honestly wasn't trying to attract Hez's attention away from Simms by talking. That was the farthest thing from my mind. I was trying to find out as much as I could from a guy I thought was plain dumb. I forgot all about Johnny Simms and the flashlight in his back pocket, and his fingers spread close to that flash. I forgot all about the fact that he'd once been a Marine, and I forgot what he'd done to Planett and his deputies when he hadn't even been angry. I forgot, too, how much he loved Lois.

I should have remembered those things.

"I ain't no sucker," Hez said. "The girl's dead and gone. Ain't nobody ever gonna know we done it."

"Who?" I said. "What girl?"

"Why, the prosty-tute," Hez said. "Lois. Who'd you think?"

There was a sudden gasp beside me, and then a deadly cold silence. I remembered Simms then, but I remembered too late.

The flashlight went on suddenly, throwing harsh blinding light onto Hez's face. And then Simms leaped and the shotgun went off. The flashlight spilled to the ground, rolling in a crazy pattern of uncontrolled light. Hez swore and tried to fire again, but Simms had his hands on his throat. I dropped to the ground, trying to get at Hez, trying to help Simms, and Hez kicked out suddenly, catching me in the groin. I yelled and rolled over, and I heard Simms say, "You son of a bitch, you lousy son of a bitch!" and all the while his hands were tightening on Hez's throat.

Hez dropped the shotgun, and his fist dug into the dungaree pocket, and I knew he was reaching for the Smith and Wesson, and then the gun barged into sight and it took Hez about four seconds to figure out how to release the safety, and then there was an explosion and Johnny Simms bucked with the shocking power of it, but he did not release Hez's throat.

Hez brought the gun up, trying for a shot at Simms' head. But Simms clutched his throat and slammed Hez's head back against the ground and the gun left Hez's hands, and Simms tightened his fingers on the leathery throat, his thumbs on the big man's Adam's apple.

They teach Marines to kill, and Johnny Simms wasn't playing. Johnny Simms was carrying a .38 caliber slug in his abdomen, but he'd just learned that his girl had been murdered. And maybe he'd attacked enemy soldiers with such ferocity, but I doubted it.

Hez tried to roll over. His eyes were beginning to bulge out of their sockets, and there was a prayer on his mouth, or a gasp, or a curse. He never got it out. His eyes rolled upward, and he tried a last stand effort to free his throat from Simms' hands, but Simms would not let go. Hez rattled, a deep rattle that started down in his bowels and shuddered up the length of his body and then trembled from between his lips like a cold wind. And then he suddenly relaxed, and he was still, and I said, "That's enough, Johnny."

Johnny Simms didn't answer me.

Johnny's hands were still tight around Hez's throat, and the blood spilled from Johnny's belly where the revolver had ripped him open at close range. I felt for his heart. He was dead.

I picked up the .38 from where it had fallen from Hez's hand. He had said the dead girl was Lois.

Then the girl who'd been put on that train this morning was Ann Grafton, and she'd been taken to Davistown.

Where in Davistown?

There was a man who might know.

17

I PUT THE .38 INTO MY JACKET POCKET, AND STARTED UP
for the car. There was a cold wind blowing in off the lake,
a wind which would speed the rain's coming. I slammed
into the convertible, started the engine, and backed out of
the court. I took the bumping medieval road doing sixty
all the way. I turned left into Sullivan's Corners and then
raced through the town, past the traffic circle, past the
blinking yellow caution light. The stars had deserted the
sky long ago. The clouds were rolling in, in bunches,
piling up like hordes of black sheep. In the distance, I
heard the solemn roll of thunder, saw the answering feeble
spit of lightning.

I pushed the gas pedal down to the floorboards when I
hit the highway. The speedometer climbed to eighty. The
thunder and lightning were moving closer now, coming in
with the sudden fury of a summer storm. You could smell
dust in the air, whirling dust, and the heavy pregnancy
that comes before water bursts from the womb of the sky.
It was going to rain like hell. It was going to wash the
town of Sullivan's Corners clean of blood.

The lone headlight appeared magically behind me, like
a Cyclops' eye in a black-masked face. I heard the wail of
the siren, and I kept my foot pressed to the accelerator
because now I knew that Ann was in serious trouble and
nothing was going to stop me, not Planett and his flunkies,
not the state cops, not the militia.

He pulled alongside on his motorcycle.

"Pull over!" he shouted.

"Screw you!" I shouted back.

The state academy had trained him well. He pulled his gun from its holster, and he rested his right hand on his left forearm, the left hand holding the bike on the road in a speeding, unswerving straight line.

"I'll fire in three seconds," he yelled.

I jammed on the brakes, and the car screeched to a skidding halt. The motorcycle pulled in beside me. By the time Fred got off the seat, I'd rolled over, yanked the .38 from my pocket, and pointed it straight at his head. He looked up into the muzzle of the Smith and Wesson. His own gun was in his hand, ready. We faced each other across the narrow blued barrels.

"Have you had to fire that since you've been a cop?" I asked.

"What?"

"Have you had to fire that gun?" I shouted.

"No."

"Neither have I. One of us'll have to in the next few minutes, Fred. I'm not going to jail again, and I'm not being stopped. Now how about it?"

The rain started. The thunder blasted the sky, and the lightning crackled in yellow-white luminescence. The drops were huge and heavy. They poured down in buckets, and we stood facing each other over the guns.

"You're a crazy bastard," Fred shouted over the roar of the thunder. "Why didn't you get out of this when you still could?"

"I still can," I said. "No more bullshit, Fred. Either you turn your bike around and head in the other direction, or I start blasting."

"You wouldn't shoot," he said. "You've got nothing to gain by—"

"NO MORE BULLSHIT!" I shouted. "Get on that bike and take off!"

"You crazy bastard! Do you think you can buck all of us? Do you think—?"

I fired.

I caught him in the shoulder, and the slug spun him around, and then his own gun went off into the air, and he crumpled to the pavement alongside his bike, the head-light still peering wakefully into the darkness. I didn't even look at him. I slid over behind the wheel. I didn't put the top up. I threw the car into gear and started off again. My hands were shaking. My foot was trembling on the gas pedal. The rain whipped the windshield, poured steadily into the car. I almost missed Handy's log cabin. My foot leaped to the brake pedal, and the wheels screeched and skidded, and I held the wheel tightly until the car side-whipped to a stop. I backed up and climbed out, leaving the motor running. I was drenched. I went to the door of Handy's cabin. This time, all the lights were out. I banged on the door with the butt of the .38.

"Who is it?" Handy called from inside.

"Colby! Open this goddamn door!"

"Just a minute, just a minute."

I waited. I rapped again to hurry him up. I was ready to shoot the door off its hinges when it opened. Handy was in pajamas and robe. I didn't bother with polite cor-dialities.

"Where's Ann Grafton?" I said, and then I shoved the gun into his belly.

"Are you out of your mind?" Handy said. "Banging on the door at this hour of the morning! Waving a gun around as if . . . "

I eased him into the room and slammed the door behind me.

"Where's Ann?" I said.

"I don't know where the hell she—"

"Two men had been shot with this gun, Handy. One is dead, and the other's lying wounded in the middle of the highway. Do you want to be number three?"

"Don't threaten me, Colby," Handy said calmly. "Guns don't scare me."

"What *does*, Handy? Look, I'm nervous. I'm over-wrought. I'm tense. I'm soaking wet. This is liable to ex-plode with no effort at all. *Where's Ann?*"

"I don't know," and he started to turn his back on me.

I spun him around. "You do know, you spineless bastard! You've known from the beginning. *Where is she?*"

Indignation flared in Handy's eyes. "Don't say that again, Colby."

"Say what, Handy? I said a lot of things."

"You know what I mean."

"The spineless part? Is that what troubles you?"

"I warned you not to . . ."

"What the hell *are* you, if not spineless? When's the last time you stood up straight? When's the last time . . . ?"

"Don't go bucking a machine, Colby! Only a fool bucks a machine."

"What machine? A sheriff and a couple of deputies? A hick state trooper on a motor bike? A couple who run a whorehouse? Is this your big machine?"

"What difference does it make how big the machine is, if it runs the town?"

"Are they what you're afraid of? Somebody told me you used to have spunk. Said you used to be a fighter. What the hell happened to you? Did you get too interested in the big payoff?"

"It's not that. I don't need the money. I—"

"All right, Handy, listen to me. I know a girl named Lois was killed. I know she was buried by Barter and Hezekiah. I know Ann was taken on a train to Davistown this morning, and I'm pretty damn sure I know why."

"They'll let her go," Handy said. "They said they'd let her go."

"Will they? A cop friend of mine went out to that motel early tonight. From what Hezekiah said, they tumbled to him. They're probably holding him, too. Do you really think they'll let him and Ann go? Damnit, Handy, they're trying to cover a murder!"

"I . . . I don't know what to think."

"Where is she?"

"I don't know." He paused. "You saw Hezekiah tonight?"

"For the last time. He's dead. A man named Johnny

Simms killed him. He killed him because he found out about Lois. He was going to marry that girl, Handy.''

"How'd this get so complicated?" Handy asked.

I didn't answer.

"How'd it get so complicated?" he asked again. "It was simple. It was . . . well, what harm were we doing? Who were we hurting?" He looked into my eyes. "Who was I hurting, Colby?"

"Yourself," I answered.

Handy lowered his head and his eyes.

"Where is she, Handy?" I asked.

Handy heaved a great sigh. "At Joe Carlisle's place," he said. "In Davistown."

"Where?"

He hesitated for a long time, and then he stood erect, with his shoulders back and he said, "I'll take you there. Let me dress."

"Throw on a coat," I said. "There may not be time for you to—"

"All right," he answered.

"Get a blanket, too," I said. "My front seat is a little damp."

Handy went into the other room. When he returned, he had taken off the robe and put on an English-cut raincoat. He was carrying a plaid blanket over his arm. We went outside. The rain had let up a little. I put up the top, spread the blanket over the soaked leather seat, and then pulled away from the cabin.

"A man's got to do the right thing eventually," Handy said.

"If he's a man," I answered. "Which way?"

"Straight through Sullivan's Corners. I'll show you from there."

"Is it a long drive?"

"About a half-hour. Be careful in Sullivan's Corners. We wouldn't want to run into Planett."

"Planett is out of commission. So's Fred. The machine is breaking down, Handy."

"I didn't know that," he said. He paused. "I offered to take you to Davistown before I knew that, Colby."

"Yes."

"I was only reminding myself," he said.

We drove through Sullivan's Corners.

"Straight ahead," Handy said, "to the next stop light. Then make a right. That road leads into Davistown."

The stop light was red when we got to it. We didn't stop. I made the right turn, and then pushed down on the accelerator.

"What happened at the motel?" I asked.

"It's complicated."

"We've got a half-hour."

"All right. You know it's a brothel?"

"Yes."

"It's a good business. It was good even before Stephanie married Barter. I mean, it was steady. Nothing high-tone, you understand. Then Stephanie imported quality. Quality meant higher prices. A $500,000 business is nothing to laugh at."

"No, it isn't."

"A business like that needs protection. You know. You're a cop."

"Yes."

"We've got a State's Attorney who's a crusader. If you want to keep something like this away from state law, you make sure the local law is in your pocket. Stephanie made sure of that. I don't know which of us she reached first. Probably Fred, probably on a small scale. Planett must have been an easy mark, too. Me . . . I don't suppose I gave her much trouble, either."

"Go on."

"You have to understand Stephanie. She's a strange girl. She wants things. She wants luxury. Prostitution is all she knows, and she's built it into a tremendous operation. She'd have succeeded in any business, do you know that? Anything she went into. She happened to choose prostitution. Or, actually, from what I gather about her background, *it chose her*. She needed capital, she got it. She married Barter who's pretty well-off, owns a good deal of property at the Point. And, of course, he had the business already and she had ideas about what she could do to that business, how she could make it *really* pay. She succeeded, too. You have to hand it to her.''

"I want to know what happened on the night of June 3rd," I said.

"I'm getting to that. It doesn't make sense, unless you know Stephanie. She's a strange girl, I told you. I've never known her not to keep her word, not to stick to a bargain. She married Barter, and she was damn good-looking when she did, you can believe me. Life hadn't been exactly gentle with her, but a beautiful girl doesn't take the hard knocks as badly. She was a beauty. Still is, for that matter, but there was this freshness about her then. Mike Barter had got himself a prize. Of course, Stephanie had got what she wanted, too. That was their bargain. No love involved, you understand. But a bargain. Stephanie keeps a bargain. And she expects the other person to keep it too. She was Barter's wife. She performed the way a wife should. She entertained, she went to bed with him, she was true to him. She was a wife. And maybe that's love, too, I don't know. Maybe that's what love adds up to.''

"And Barter?"

"You've met him, haven't you?"

"Yes."

"He's not what I'd call a . . . watch it, there's something in the road.''

I swerved the car around a branch that had been knocked loose by the storm. The rain had almost ended. The windshield wipers snicked at scattered drops.

"He's not what I'd call a Hollywood type he-man," Handy said. "In fact, he's pretty ugly. Do you agree?"

"I suppose."

"You'd think a man like Barter . . . with a woman like Stephanie, well, you'd think he'd be pretty happy, wouldn't you?"

"Yes."

"Last night . . . something happened.''

"What?"

"The girl Lois was in cabin eleven. That's not too far from the office. Barter went out for a walk. Stephanie was alone up at the office. She was probably playing her records. She's got a lot of records, likes to play them. I mean, really a lot. I guess she never had a Victrola when she was a kid, never could afford one. She was probably playing her records when she heard a scream. She called for Barter first, then realized he wasn't in the office."

"What time was this?"

"About eight or so, I guess. It was just getting dark, from the way I got it. I wasn't there, you understand. Stephanie told me all this later. On the phone."

"Go on."

"She keeps a gun, Stephanie. A beautiful woman like her . . . out at the Point there . . . she keeps a gun. She's a beautiful woman, you know."

"I know," I said. There was something odd in Handy's voice whenever he spoke of Stephanie.

"And noble," he said, "and—despite what you may think—pure. You can't use a dirty word in her presence. You just can't. She's that way."

"Go on, Handy."

"She took the gun . . . a .32, I think it is, I'm not sure, and she went outside. There was screaming from cabin eleven. She knew the girl was in there alone. She thought maybe an animal or something had wandered in there, frightening her. She went to the cabin." Handy paused, and then he sighed.

"Yes?"

"An animal *had* wandered into the cabin. The animal was Mike Barter."

"Oh."

"Stephanie threw open the door and found him struggling with the girl. It's funny with prostitutes, Colby. This wasn't business with Barter. This was something else, and Lois didn't want it, and she fought him like a tigress. And Stephanie stood in the doorway with the gun in her hand and then—the way it can happen—without will, without reason, without logic, she was firing. She fired four times." Handy sucked in his breath. "She killed the girl."

"Why?"

Handy nodded. "You'd think she'd have killed Barter. He was the one who'd cheated her. But maybe a woman turns instinctively against the other woman, maybe it's bred into her. And maybe in the heat of emotion you seek the natural enemy, and the natural enemy here was the other woman. And then she saw the girl fall, and all at once everything was drained out of her. She'd killed someone. She dropped the gun, and she would have bolted from the cabin, but Barter stopped her. He picked up the gun and stuck it in his pocket. Then he dragged the girl into the cabin closet. She was bleeding pretty badly, and he had to get her out of the way while he thought of something."

"What did he think of?"

"He got Hezekiah, and together they moved the body into the truck. They covered the girl with a burlap sack, and they drove the truck into the woods. They would have buried her right then and there, I guess, but they didn't want to bury her anywhere on the property, and they had to figure out just where they *could*. They went back to the office. They were probably talking it over when you pulled up with your girl."

"I see."

"Barter never would've rented you a cabin, if you hadn't had the girl with you. He's a quick thinker. He probably went to look at your girl only because he's got an eye for the women. But when he saw her, he knew just what he'd do. Lois was a tall brunette. Your girl was about the same height, same general build, pretty. Lois wasn't too well known in town, just been here a few days, and in the cabin with customers most of the time. He knew sooner or later somebody'd come looking for Lois. Girl can't just disappear without somebody coming to find out why. He didn't want snoopers. Snoopers might call in state law. State law would mean the end of the setup."

"I can take it from there," I said.

"Can you?"

"While I was in the shower, he explained the plan to Stephanie and Hez. They grabbed Ann out of the cabin, took the truck out of the woods, and then drove her some place for the night."

"Hez's place," Handy said.

"In the morning, Stephanie put on something that would attract attention. Blanche *always* attracts attention. The three of them went to town together. Blanche is a known prostitute, Stephanie a known madam. People would automatically assume the brunette was one of the girls. People would assume the brunette was Lois. So if anyone asked questions later on, the answer would be that Lois had left town. Hell, everyone saw her go."

"Yes. But they planned on turning Ann free, I'm sure they did."

"Maybe that was part of the plan originally, but once they'd found out I was a cop, once they'd thought it over, how *could* they turn her free? Damnit, Handy, she may be dead already!"

"I . . . I don't think so." He peered through the windshield. "We're entering Davistown now. It's just a little way further."

The rain had stopped. I turned off the windshield wipers. The roads were still slickly wet, and they told their secrets to the tires of the car.

"How long have you loved her, Handy?" I asked.

"What?"

"Stephanie."

Without hesitation, Handy said, "From the first day Mike Barter brought her to Sullivan's Point."

"Why are you leading me to her?"

This time, Handy hesitated. I thought he wasn't going to answer at all. Then he said, "I used to be a good lawyer. I used to be a good justice of the peace, too. I used to believe in the law." He paused. "Stephanie killed someone." He paused again. "I imagine *that* person was loved, too."

Davistown was an ugly city, ugly with smokestacks and gaudy neon and pool parlors and second-rate bars. We drove into it, and Handy directed me to a three-story apartment building on the fringe of the downtown area.

A light was burning in a third-floor apartment. The rest of the building was in bed.

"What's the apartment number?" I asked.

"I don't know. His name is Joe Carlisle."

"You wait here, Handy."

"Be careful," he said, and he sounded as if he meant it.

I got out of the convertible. The street was very quiet. In the lobby of the building, I checked the mailboxes. There was a Joseph Carlisle in apartment 33. I brought my foot up and kicked the snap lock on the inner door. The door sprang open, and I found the stairs and took them up to the third floor. Apartment 33 was at the end of the hall. I pulled out the .38, released the safety, and knocked.

"Who is it?" Stephanie asked.

"Hezekiah," I whispered.

"Hold on."

I heard her approaching the door. The door opened a crack then, and I saw surprise and shock come into her eyes. She tried to slam the door shut, and she yelled something to somebody in the apartment, but I'd already flung my shoulder at the door. I shoved it open, and Stephanie reeled backwards, lost her footing, and fell to the floor. Barter and Carlisle came rushing from the other room. They stopped dead when they saw me, and then the trapped look came into their eyes, and their feet stood undecided, and their hands fluttered somewhat aimlessly, and then their shoulders slumped because they were facing a .38 and a murder rap, and there was no place to go.

"Who told you where we were?" Stephanie said from the floor. Her eyes were puzzled. She was watching her dream collapse around her, watching the thick carpets and the hi-fi unit and the liquor cabinet crumble into the dust.

"It doesn't matter," I said. "Get up."

And then the girl who didn't like to hear profanity

looked up at me, and her eyes filled with tears, and she
said, "You bastard, you dirty rotten bastard."

And that was all.

It was quiet in the squad room of the 23rd Precinct.
There was July sunlight filtering through the meshed windows that opened on the street. Tony Mitchell and Sam
Thompson sat at one of the desks. There were two coffee
cups before them. Mitchell drank steadily. Thompson did
not drink as often because he was talking. He did not like
to occupy his mouth with too many tasks at the same time.

"You can always tell a hero cop from a plain ordinary
bull," he said.

"Can you?" Mitchell asked, smiling.

"Certainly. You're a cop with heroic dimensions. I can
tell."

"How can you tell?"

"It's very simple. In all the years I've been on the force,
I have never met a single cop who got bit by a snake. You
are unique."

"I never met one, either."

"Which only proves my point. You're a white hunter!
Tony, you are a hero!"

"Phil's the hero. He's the one who cracked it."

"Tony, the one who cracks it is not the hero. The one
who *gets* cracked is the hero. Look at yourself! God, how
can you stand looking so pathetically wounded? A Band-
Aid on your leg, your head in a bandage. Your wife must
be dissolving in sympathy."

"She gives me breakfast in bed every morning. Bite
size."

"Predigested, she should give you."

"It won't last long," Mitchell said sorrowfully. "The
bandage comes off my head tomorrow."

"The white hunter!" Thompson said, carried away with
himself. "Look at him! Fearless! Indomitable! Honest!
Jesus, I can hardly stand it."

Phil Colby pushed his way through the railing which
divided the squad room from the corridor outside. He

walked directly to a chair near the desk, plopped into it, stretched his legs, and said, "Any more coffee?"

"What are you doing back here?" Thompson asked. "Is the trial over?"

"It's over," Colby said. "Isn't there any more coffee?"

"O'Hare has a pot brewing next door. You want some?"

"I'd like some."

"O'Hare!" Thompson yelled. "A cup of coffee for the returning hero."

"What happened?" Mitchell asked.

"The D.A. got a conviction."

"Good."

"Yeah." Colby sighed. "That courtroom was hot, you know?"

"That's why I let you solve the thing," Mitchell said.

"Why?"

"I don't like testifying before district attorneys. Especially in the summertime."

"You're noble," Colby said. He turned to look toward the corridor. "Hey, O'Hare," he yelled. "You coming with that coffee?"

O'Hare came into the squad room, his shirt sleeves rolled up to the elbows. He was carrying a pot of coffee in one hand and two cups in the other.

"I wanted to finish a report I was on," he said, grinning. "This way I can join you." He put the cups down on the desk. He poured coffee into both of them. "Pass that container of milk, Tony," he said.

Mitchell passed the milk. Thompson passed the sugar. O'Hare administered both to his coffee. Then he sipped it, made a satisfied "Ahhh" with his mouth, smiled and said, "So what's new with the star witness?"

And Phil Colby picked up his coffee cup and said, "So what could be new?"